MAGIC

Coeur du Bayou Trilogy
Book Three

LISA COOTS

This is a work of fiction. Names, characters, businesses, places, events and incidents are either the products of the author's imagination or used in a fictitious manner.

Any resemblance to actual persons, living or dead, or actual events is purely coincidental.

Solunapublishing.com

P.O. Box 775
Jennings, LA 70546

ISBN: 0-9907669-6-9
ISBN-13: 978-0-9907669-6-4

Cover Art: Phycel Designs, Inc.
phycel.com

DEDICATION

To my Sun, Dwayne.

*Your music will always
call to my soul.*

*And to my stars,
Asa, Toni, and Emily,
my reasons for living.*

*You all have brought joy
and magic to my life.*

All my love, always.

FORGOTTEN MEMORIES

Leaves rustle in the distance
mixed with familiar strains of music
floating gently on the wind.
Pulling at my heart
like a violin string drawn by a gypsy's bow.
The world stopped,
all was frozen but the breeze.
There I stood posing for a portrait,
hand on hip, skirt billowing at my knees.
I was her and she was me,
a proud dark eyed gypsy woman.
Was it just a dream
or a forgotten memory?

Lisa Coots
Sept. 1992

CHAPTER 1

"I'm her husband. Who the hell are you?"

"What?" a chorus of surprised voices echoed in the darkness around Serena. She tried unsuccessfully to steady the dancing flame she held in her shaking hand. The unexpected appearance of Richie's ghost had rattled her. Serena hadn't felt the stranger's nearness. Except he wasn't a stranger to her.

"Husband?" Claire's terrified voice asked from the shadows at the top of the stairs.

"No, you're not," Serena spat defiantly over the candle.

"Then why are you using my name?" Even in the darkness she could hear the amusement in his voice. The same voice that haunted her dreams.

"I like it better than mine." Her casual shrug and

flippant answer invoked a chuckle from the newcomer.

"Hate to interrupt the reunion, guys," Ben spoke up never taking his eyes off the gadget in his hand, "but those were some major readings."

"Rena, what's going on here?" His smooth deep voice edged with concern as he took in the attire of the group. Still dressed for the engagement party, her friends remained rooted where they stood when the electricity had gone off.

"None of your business. How did you even find me?" The question in her head popped out of her mouth even though she knew the answer.

"Three years I've been looking for you. Three years... Then I come across a file on Ben's desk and find out you've been practically in my backyard this whole time." The pain, resentment, and even a hint of accusation in his voice was not lost on her.

"Hey, she just contacted me a month ago. I had no idea where she was before that." Ben's calm matter of fact tone was one he used often to diffuse tense situations. Serena wasn't sure how successful it would be tonight.

A whimper from Claire reminded Serena that everyone was still there, watching the scene in the dim light. Their curiosity obviously kept them quiet, but upon hearing Claire, Evan pushed Ben out of his way and bounded up the stairs. With an arm wrapped around her, he carefully escorted Claire back down, their shadows growing behind them as they descended.

"If you're ok, we'll leave you guys to sort this out." His statement was directed at Serena, but Evan's dark eyes watched her friends warily.

She nodded silently, torn between wanting them all to leave and the fear of being left alone.

"Wait. You're married?" Claire stepped away from Evan to search her friend's face. "You never told us."

Thunder rumbled outside, and Serena could feel the tension thicken in the air around her.

"Somebody tell me what's going on here," demanded the man claiming to be her husband.

"We're all kinda in the dark here, pal." Jake stated the obvious.

"Claire, are you alright?" Serena ignored their exchange to focus on Claire.

"Was it really Richie?" Her voice trembled as she looked to her friends. At a loss for words, Jake and Faith shrugged.

"Yes." Serena answered for them. "He's been making his presence known."

"What?" Evan's eyes widened in disbelief. "Why didn't you say something?"

"I knew you wouldn't believe me and I didn't want to ruin this for Claire, or Faith." She looked back at Faith, who stood half hidden in shadows, not sure what else to say.

Faith nodded in understanding. "Evan, just go on and take Claire home."

Serena felt all eyes on her. The candle only added heat to her flushed face as she gazed around the foyer at her friends. She had come to love and care for them like family, but they really didn't know her. Would they feel differently once they knew the truth? She had taken a chance calling Ben, but things had become crazy. Richie was angry at her. This was different because it was so personal. She felt she needed help, and Ben, in the short time she had known him, had been a good friend. She figured Mason would find her eventually. Calling Ben had guaranteed their reunion. Thinking she was ready to face him once again, she made the call. Judging by her shaking hand, and quaking insides, maybe she wasn't ready after all.

"Maybe they should all leave and you can tell me what's going on?" Mason lowered his voice patiently.

"Of course. Y'all should go. You, too." She smiled at him, desperately trying to appear calm. "There's no point in staying. I can handle it."

"Obviously you can't or you would have never called Ben for help." Serena opened her mouth to argue, but he cut her off. "I can feel them. I'm not going anywhere."

The glint in his eyes shimmered in the candlelight. Serena had seen that look before. There was no denying or downplaying the activity. He was like her. The reason she thought, at one time, they were meant to be together. She had been wrong. So very wrong, and it hurt. It hurt to look at him and remember everything.

The lights flickered then flooded them all in brightness. Serena squinted and blinked. All eyes were now on Mason; whose eyes were still on her. His muscular build was not hidden by the damp, plain clothing. His dark bangs fell into green-gold eyes. His hair had been longer last time she saw him. Memories of his long raven colored mane tickling her body during their lovemaking made her break out in a new layer of sweat. Still not as close cropped as Ben kept his, this shorter style suited Mason.

"I'll help you finish cleaning up." Faith looked to Serena then nodded to the newcomer with a raised brow.

"Oh, sorry. Everyone, this is Mason Del Toro, an old acquaintance of mine."

"Ouch," Jake muttered under his breath.

Mason pursed his lips, nodding to the group gathered around Serena. "We can discuss titles later, Rena. We'll have plenty of time for that. This house is an amazing find."

Now with the lights on he turned to take in the foyer and staircase. To everyone else, he was just admiring the house. She knew better.

His gazed wandered back to the group and fixed on Faith. He smiled widely.

"Ahhhh." He closed his eyes and sighed. "Love."

"Stop it," Serena hissed.

"And sadness. So much sadness."

Everyone watched in awkward silence, Mason's face clearly showing the emotion he was feeling.

"Hmm. Curious." Mason stepped closer to the staircase, and put a hand out.

"I said stop."

The first step creaked as he put his weight on it slowly. He paused there, hand gripping the newel post. "Ah. So recent and angry." His eyes closed again as he breathed in deeply. His eyes popped open and found Serena.

"Oh, Rena. What have you done?"

CHAPTER 2

"Hey." Ben's concerned voice drifted through the opening of the sliding door before hesitantly shouldering his way through.

"What?" Serena didn't bother to look at him. She had fled to the big room under the pretense of cleaning up. Unable to bear the looks from her friends, she planned to hide out here until they were all gone. Not bothering with the lights, she stacked chairs by candlelight.

"I have him settled upstairs. Not in the front room like you asked." He hesitated a breath, when she didn't face him he continued, "You sure you don't want me to stay down here with you?"

"Yes, Ben." She sighed finally turning toward him. "I'll be fine down here. Everyone else gone?"

"Yeah. They were worried about you. They're good friends, Serena."

"For now." She rolled her eyes and sighed again. "Once they know everything that will change. It always does."

"Not always. I still feel the same about you, so does…"

"Stop," she interrupted him, not needing to be reminded of Mason and his feelings. "Did you leave the file for him to find?"

"No." He shook his head. "If he even had an inkling that I knew where you were… It doesn't surprise me that he went through my desk."

"I don't want him here." The lie echoed off of the walls of the now empty room.

"Serena, you called me for help. I'm here and frankly, this place is incredible. The things you have recorded here over the last year show more activity than any case I've ever seen. And what happened tonight in front of so many witnesses, that's unheard of." The excitement in his voice was rare. Normally a skeptic, she could tell he was thrilled at the experiences. His face shone like a kid on Christmas morning.

"He's not leaving, and you know it." Ben shook his head again then looked her straight in the eyes. "He won't let this go, and he can't let you go."

"That might not be something he can control."

He looked around the cleared room thoughtfully, then he nodded towards the narrow opening of the doors. "Should I close this all the way?"

"No, leave it. That's fine."

"Holler if anything else happens."

"It's been an eventful evening. I think it'll be quiet for a while."

Ben nodded again then slipped back through the opening, leaving her alone.

The stress of the party, having everyone here while knowing Richie was lurking in the shadows left her drained but restless. The restless part she knew had more to do with Mason.

She pushed the last standing table up against the wall and put the music on low. Her escape had always been music. The flow of the melody moved her soul, forcing her body to sway with the beat, slowly at first. Lifting her arms gracefully, she let the music take her. As always the freedom of movement began to release the tension in her neck and shoulders as she relaxed into the music. Her mind began to wander.

She wouldn't leave this time. Coeur du Bayou was her home. She had been dreaming of this house her whole life. She was tired of moving, and her friends were her family. They all needed this place. They were all three drawn to it. All hurting and searching, they had found each other and this place.

Claire had been wounded physically and emotionally. Running from a past that wouldn't let her go. Richie, her abusive lover from that dark past had come after her looking for stolen money. Now he was stuck here, an active, angry restless spirit. She had tried to keep it from her friends, especially Claire. Knowing how Richie had hurt her, she didn't want anything to ruin the happiness Claire had found with Evan.

Serena had noticed the sparks at their first meeting. A vision of Evan and Claire dancing together had her convinced it would work out for them. Evan was so serious and level headed it had taken him awhile to come around. Claire was so open and bubbly; she knew they would balance each other out. Turning with the music, she closed her eyes and smiled thinking of the happiness in their future.

Faith was more tightly tied to the house. The experiences she had encountered were baffling to Serena. Not the encounters per say, just that they happened to Faith and not her. Faith and Jake had more to do with the history of Coeur du Bayou. Their love had obviously triggered forgotten memories. Stepping forward into a sway of her hips, she lifted her arms again as she considered Faith and Jake. Their love was like a comforting heat that surrounded and connected them. Serena likened it to the feeling of a warm bath, comfortable, relaxing and safe. It was definitely going to last.

As the song ended she let out a sigh, still holding the pose. The next song started, a slower suggestive pace. Her hips gyrated as she lifted her arms over head. The silky material of her skirt caressed her calves, reminding her of other dances, other times. Serena had wished for him. Her perfect mate, someone like her that would understand and not push her away.

Memories of Mason and their passion burned in her, an uncontrollable fire. A passion beyond reason. She knew their love wasn't so gentle or comfortable. Instead of belonging to each other, they both burned like wildfire. Fire on fire, the heat consumed them, cancelling each other out. A hot tear fell on her face mixing with the perspiration as she moved faster with the beat. She danced hoping to wipe the hateful memories from her mind. They would serve no purpose now. Her grandmother's voice was still clear in her head. *"Careful what you wish for, girl."*

Her head fell forward as she realized Ben was right. She needed Mason's help. Other than the fact she knew she belonged here, nothing else was clear to her. Everything seemed fuzzy. Mason however, had walked in and felt it all. Like magic.

⁓⁓⁓

Mason heard the music as he descended the stairs. He knew he'd find her dancing in the big room. Why hadn't he thought to search for her through belly dancing channels? For all of her flightiness, she was a creature of habit. She would never stop dancing.

He watched her through the opening and remembered. The first time he saw her, she was dancing. That one dance had cast a spell on him. With every sway of her hips he had lost all reason, ending a two-year engagement to a logical choice of wife. It didn't matter. Passion trumped logic in his world. He knew he could spend the rest of his life watching her dance. Amid the crowd, her dark eyes had opened and found his. He saw the recognition register on her face, her lips parting in a silent gasp. She knew.

As if feeling him again, Serena turned sharply to face him, chest heaving.

"No, Mason." Her breathy plea stopped him from entering the room.

"It's ok. I've found you once again. I just had to make sure you were real." He gave her a wistful smile.

She hung her head, dark curls falling over her

face.

"It took you long enough." He heard her faint whisper over the music.

"I was looking for you in the sand, not the swamp. Good night, Rena."

Her head snapped up at his reply. Mason watched the memories play across her face as he closed the door. He would leave her alone for now. It was enough to know he wouldn't be the only one reliving those memories tonight, like he did every night.

CHAPTER 3

Mason woke with a start, gasping for breath in the unfamiliar room. The weight on his chest pinning him to the bed.

"No!" In his barely conscious state, the yell from his own body brought him to an upright sitting position. The bunched sheet clenched tightly in his fists on either side felt like a restraint. He willed his hands to release, loosening the sheet, and took a deep calming breath. He felt the air around him. Quiet, too quiet.

"No." He couldn't feel her. Trying not to panic, he grabbed his jeans and pulled them on quickly. His bare feet slapped the hardwood floor of the landing as he crossed to the stairs. Taking them two at time, he headed for the voices coming from the kitchen. She was gone again.

Ben looked up in surprise from his seat at the island counter as Mason burst into the bright, roomy kitchen.

"Where is she?"

"Who?" The startled female voice took him by surprise. The dark haired woman from the night before stood near the stove watching him.

"You..."

"Me? You're looking for me?" Her hand nervously grabbed at the front of her apron.

"No. Serena. She's gone." It was a statement, not a question. He knew she was gone.

"Oh, she just ran out. She'll be back."

"Ran out?" His voice cracked as he took a step in her direction.

"Bad choice of words. She just means she went to the store. Relax, Mace. You're scaring the cook." He didn't bother to look at Ben. The scraping of his fork on the plate told Mason he was more interested in his food as always.

Mason was focused on the woman in front of him, clutching the front of her apron with a death grip.

"Breathe," he commanded.

She gulped the air in. Once. Twice. "How did you know?"

"There's so much sadness..." He closed his eyes, letting it wash over him.

"Not anymore. I don't feel it as much as before." At her soft voice, he opened his eyes to find her hand now covering her stomach.

"Where's the baby?" he demanded taking another step closer, his eyes boring into hers.

"I don't know." Her whisper was barely audible.

"Whoa…," Ben interrupted, "Can we all just get some coffee and have breakfast before we jump into it?"

"Of course. I'm sorry." Mason blinked away the feelings and tried to focus on the present. "Sometimes it takes me by surprise."

"Yeah, Mason, if you'd like to finish dressing, then we can catch up while we wait for Serena to get back." Ben waved his fork in Mason's direction.

Mason looked down at his bare chest and feet. "I'm sorry. Please forgive my manners. I must seem like a madman to you. I'm usually better behaved, but when it comes to Rena I lose my head. Your name again?"

"Faith."

"Faith," he repeated smiling. "Please excuse me. I'll get dressed and we can start over." He backed towards the door.

She smiled at him. "You call her Rena?"

"Yes."

"That's sweet." The smile disappeared as she turned back toward the stove. "Now sit and eat before it gets cold."

"I should…" Motioning to his chest, he smiled apologetically.

"No, don't bother. I won't faint, but my brother would never come to the table without a shirt on." She gave a little snort as Mason pulled out the stool next to Ben and sat.

"Eat. I've got baking to do once I clean this mess." She placed a heaping plate of eggs, bacon and toast in front of him then hurried back to the stove.

Ben shrugged, flashed a devilish smile and dove back into his food.

"Tell me," Mason urged.

"No. When Serena gets back. I haven't had a chance to talk to her. I don't know you." Glancing over her shoulder, she narrowed her eyes at them. "You're not a photographer, and you...." Brandishing the spatula in Mason's direction, she turned to face him. "You're her husband, really?"

"Actually, I am a photographer." Ben's tone was calm, but he sat up straighter letting his fork drop onto his plate.

"You're right. We should wait for Serena. If she hasn't told you about us, I'm guessing there's a reason." Mason gave her a smirk.

Faith turned back to the stove with a flip of her ponytail, obviously annoyed.

"You live here?" The smell of the food had his stomach growling. He gave in and picked up the fork.

"No, I bake here." Gathering utensils, she dropped them in the soapy water of the sink.

"There's a connection. You and this house."

"I said wait for Serena."

"Wait for Serena for what?" The bags of groceries crinkled as Serena's arms tightened around them at the sight of Mason shirtless.

"He's jumping into it." Ben glanced up briefly, then went back to his plate.

Mason got up from the counter and walked towards her. Serena's mouth went dry.

"We dress for meals around here."

"Yes, I've been made aware." He held out his arms, and she thrust the bags into them. Careful not to touch him, Serena stepped back and turned her attention to Faith.

"You didn't have to cook for them, hun. They're not guests exactly." Dreading this moment, she hesitated trying to find the words.

"I'll be happy to pay for the rooms, if that's a problem." Mason searched for a spot to put the groceries down.

"And food," Ben chimed in. "I'll pay for the food. This is great."

"No, you're here to work. I don't want your money."

"Work?" Faith grabbed a bag from Mason and started digging out the items.

"Yes, work. I'm Reuben Peltier and this is Mason Del Toro. We're paranormal investigators. Our team is called Spirit Catchers, Inc."

"Paranormal…" Hugging a jar of mayo to her, Faith processed the information. "Serena?"

"Serena worked with us for a while. We…," Mason started to explain.

"Mason," Serena warned.

"Sorry, love. I think the cat was already half out of the bag. She's connected obviously."

"You know?" The question was more of an accusation. Serena felt her anger rising.

"I just picked up some of it. We haven't really talked." Finally putting the bag on a counter, Mason turned towards her. The ease with which he stood in her kitchen, bare chested chatting with Faith irked her. With a swish of her skirt, she headed out of the kitchen.

"Rena, wait," Mason called following her into the foyer.

She stood at the open front door of her home unable to contain her irritation.

"What?" She turned to face him, anger vibrating through her.

"What is it? It's not just me being here. There's something else." His concern should have dampened her temper. Instead it fueled it.

"Not you? It is you! You walk into my house... I dreamed of this house my whole life, even before you. I found it. I bought it, and you walk in... knowing. I can't see it, not clearly. Why? Why won't it show me?"

He reached for her his face a mask of compassion.

"No, Mason." She held her hands out in front of her. "Then you... I was trying to put everything together. Start over. I had a chance here."

"Start over? Without me?" His bare chest heaved with anger. "No, Rena. We both know that's impossible. Don't keep running away. I'm going to fix this."

"By accusing me?" Her raised voice echoed through the foyer.

"What?"

"You basically accused me of pushing Richie down the stairs in front of my friends."

"No." His black bangs spilled over into his eyes as he shook his head in denial.

"Yes, you did."

"I just said what I felt." He shook his head once again as if to clear it. "He felt. He thinks you pushed him and he's not happy about it."

"That much I gathered on my own."

"I'm not leaving."

"I didn't say..."

"You didn't have to. I can see it on your face. Whatever our problems, we will work it out. I won't leave you to deal with this alone."

Being read was the last straw, her fury came out like a venomous whip. "Got a whiff of money? Or is it fame?"

The front door slammed shut, followed by another door upstairs. The air changed around her suddenly. The whiff of wet dog mixed with rotting meat invaded her nostrils. Richie.

"*Bitch.... Where's my money?*" The sickly whisper caressed her cheek.

"I don't have your money," she hissed into the air around her. "And I didn't push you."

She turned in a circle searching for the source of the voice.

Mason grabbed her arm pulling her up against him protectively. She felt the hard muscles of his chest against her back through the thin material of her shirt. The spark from their skin touching traveled through her body like a rampant wild fire. His bare arms encircled her, sending her emotions reeling.

"Did you hear that?" she asked him trying not to focus on the heat between them.

"Yes, I did." His voice so near her ear sent another seductive wave of heat down her body. When she tried to move away from him, he added, "Did you feel that?"

"Yes," she whispered stepping out of his arms.

"I'm not leaving."

"I know. Let me know when you want to set up

the equipment and I'll tell you where I've had the most activity."

He nodded, his gold eyes never leaving hers.

"Ben, finish eating we have work to do. Faith, when you have free time, I'd like to talk to you and your man." Not bothering to turn, he addressed Ben and Faith who watched from the kitchen doorway, then headed up the stairs.

Serena let out a sigh, her insides still quaking. She knew better than to let her anger flow freely. With Mason around it would be more difficult to control her emotions.

Magic was a funny thing. *Careful what you wish for, girl. Once you get it, you just have to deal with it.*

"I need to go... walk or something."

"I'll come with you." Faith quickly slipped off her apron and handed it to Ben.

"It's ok. I know you have baking to do." Not sure she was ready for the barrage of questions she tried to put Faith off once again.

"No, I need to talk to you."

"Maybe we should do this later, when Claire's here."

"No, come on." Faith took her by the arm leading her to the door. "You've got some 'splaining to do, Lucy."

She could hear Ben chuckling behind them. Faith opened the door and pushed her out into the sticky Louisiana summer heat. Serena drew in a deep breath of pine, to clear the lingering stench of Richie.

Once they were down the path, Faith finally spoke up.

"Serena, what's going on?"

"You were there. You saw."

"Yeah, I saw what I assumed was Richie last night. That doesn't explain everything else. Ben? Mason? Are you married?"

"No, we're not actually married. We did talk about it, but things didn't work out."

"So you worked with them on the paranormal stuff?"

The determined look on Faith's face told Serena she wasn't getting away without all of the details. This was it. The conversation she had hoped she'd never have with her friends.

"Yeah, I can sense things, like they can. It's not always like this though. Faith, you have to understand. I didn't come here for this. I dreamed about this house for years. When things didn't work out with Mason, suddenly here it was. I found it when I needed it, just like magic. I belong here. I didn't mean to keep anything from you and Claire. My life before didn't seem relevant. I never thought you'd be pulled into this…." She searched for the right word to describe everything that had happened and came up empty. Her hands had been moving in jerky arcs as she talked, now dropped lifelessly to her sides. "You know."

Narrowing her eyes at Serena, Faith considered for a moment. Her mouth twitched into a smirk.

"What?" Waiting for the judgements and accusations, she steadied herself.

"So what's your real last name?"

Laughing heartily at the unexpected question, she felt some of the weight lifted. Faith's wittiness was one of the reasons she loved having her around.

"That's what you want to know? It's Klump." Watching for Faith's reaction, she wasn't disappointed.

"Oh yeah, I'd rather Del Toro, too. Sounds exotic." She lifted her eyebrows then dropped them again. "Just a warning though, Evan was pretty freaked out."

"I know. Everyone was. I half expected him to show up first thing this morning to interrogate me."

"It's still early." Faith snorted.

"I really expected Claire to show up, too."

"Evan probably won't let her out of his sight."

"What about Jake?"

"Jake knows what's going on. I don't think any of us understand it, but this house means a lot to us, too."

They reached the small graveyard, long forgotten, until Claire had literally tripped over it while hiding from Richie last Halloween.

"He knew. Mason knew about her baby. How?" Faith's voice was filled with amazement and her dark eyes looked to Serena for answers.

"He can sense things."

"Yeah, but I had to tell you after I saw it. He knew."

"It's different for each of us. Sometimes things are clear for me and not him. Here, he seems to be picking up on everything."

"So what's next?"

"I'm hoping he can help. They have equipment. EVP recordings sometimes pick up voices." Serena ran a hand over a headstone thinking about Richie. "Richie was just loud and clear. Did you hear him?"

"No, but I figured it was him. I heard what you said. Was last night the first time?"

"No... Well, the first time I've seen him."

"Why didn't you tell us?"

"I didn't want to upset Claire. She's finally happy. I thought maybe I could figure it out, so she'd be rid of him for good. That's why I called Ben for help."

"So none of it's over? Richie, the mystery lady or her missing baby?"

Serena shook her head sadly. "No, I don't think so."

Faith pulled at the long grass next to a headstone. "Have you always been like this?"

"Yes." Not ready to talk about her life and insecurities, she ran a hand over the head stone. "Do you feel anything here?"

Faith looked up in surprise, a wad of grass in her hands.

"No, it's always in the house." As if to test, she dropped the grass, wiped her hands on her jeans then touched the headstone. "No, nothing…"

"Let's head back. It's getting hot out here."

"Ok. Are you sure you're ok with all of this?"

"What do you mean?"

"You're always so calm, but I can tell this is getting to you."

"Faith. Come on. I'll be fine. I just don't want anything to mess up our business plans. People are attracted to haunted places, but Richie is so angry he could scare people away."

"Oh, no. We can't let that happen. Can Ben and Mason help us get rid of him?"

"I'm betting on it. That's the only reason I'm letting Mason stay."

"Hmm… I don't read people, but I know there's more between you two." Faith glanced slyly at Serena as they walked back down the path. She stopped suddenly grabbing Serena's arm excitedly. "What if he's connected to the house too? Like me. That's why he can sense things. Have you considered that?"

The thought stunned her. Not only had she not considered it, the thought had never occurred to her. No, it couldn't be. As closely as they were tied already, if he was also involved in the mystery of the house, she'd never be rid of him. Coeur du Bayou was hers. She wouldn't even entertain the thought that he could take it from her.

CHAPTER 4

Serena heard the raised voices before she saw Evan's cruiser in the driveway.

"Oh, no!" Faith picked up her pace and hurried ahead.

Tempted to turn back or sneak in through the back door, Serena continued on. After Mason's demonstration on the stairs, she knew she'd have some questions to answer. The cop in Evan wouldn't be able to let it go.

As she reached the porch, Evan's voice was loud and clear. "Damn it, Faith! Go home!"

"Evan, stop it." Hands on her hips, Faith was holding her ground.

"I'm not sure your presence is needed here, officer." Blocking the doorway, Mason now fully dressed crossed his arms, his tone dismissive.

"Deputy." Evan corrected.

"Ah, yes, labels..." She could hear the amusement in Mason's voice and cringed.

"Where's Serena?" Evan demanded.

"I'm not sure I like your tone, deputy. What exactly is the nature of your business here?"

"Mason. Stop." Serena warned climbing the steps quickly.

"I could ask you the same thing." Evan leaned in mincingly towards Mason.

"Cut it out. Both of you." Pushing her way between them, she faced Evan. "Is there a problem?"

"I need to talk to you. Alone." He looked past her to glare at Mason.

Before Mason could reply, she warned him. "Not your house. Remember that. These people are my friends. They are always welcome here."

"As you wish." His gold eyes flashed with anger, before he turned on his heel. "We're setting up in the upstairs room. Faith, remember I need to talk to you."

"No..." Evan's protest was immediate, so was Faith's reaction.

"Hello? Grown up, remember?" She added an eye roll for good measure then answered Mason, "I'll come by with Jake tonight if he can get away. I've got to get in the kitchen."

"Come on." Serena motioned towards the parlor. "Is this room ok, or should we go in my office?"

"Huh?" Evan frowned at Mason's back then followed her into the parlor.

"You said it was private."

"Oh yeah, I need to know what's going on here. Who is that guy to you?" Jerking a thumb towards the foyer, he paced nervously.

"What?" Shocked at his concern, her heart warmed. She had expected his visit but had assumed he'd be questioning her past, especially after hearing she wasn't using her real name.

"Look, you've been a good friend to Claire, and Faith. This guy.... I don't know. Something doesn't feel right."

"Please sit, Evan."

"Is he your husband?" Ignoring her request, he paced keeping an eye on the doorway.

"No," she answered truthfully, then added, "not in this life."

"So if you want him to leave, just say." Not actually hearing her, his hands fisted at his sides. "I'll make him go."

"Thanks, but honestly, I think I need his help."

"With what?"

"Richie. You saw him last night. I know you did. You can't pretend that didn't happen. You and I both know it was him. We saw him last Halloween. He died on that staircase."

"Exactly. How could it be him?" Sitting heavily on the sofa, he finally looked at her.

"Evan, I know you don't want to believe any of this. Believe me, I wish I had that luxury."

"I'm sorry. I want to help you, but if I let myself believe that was Richie last night, standing behind Claire." He shook his head. "I don't want her anywhere near here, her or my pigheaded sister."

"Talking shit behind my back, bro." Elle breezed

into the room, hair spiked and a sassy grin on her face.

"Ugh…. Either of my pigheaded, foul mouthed sisters." Hanging his head, Evan groaned.

Elle gave a smirk. "I just came to say goodbye to Faith. I was surprised to see you here, but two birds, one stop. I've got to get back to Dallas, but I'll be back for the wedding."

"Yeah, ok." He looked uncomfortably at Serena then hung his head again guiltily.

"No… You can't." Serena finally understood what he was trying to say.

"What? What's going on?" Elle watched them suspiciously.

"There won't be a wedding here." His words were firm as he stood and faced Serena.

"Have you lost your mind? What the hell happened after I left last night?" Elle looked from Evan to Serena, her brown eyes rounded with disbelief.

"You can't cancel the wedding. Claire will be devastated." The knot in her gut told Serena she had been right to keep Richie's presence from them.

"Does Faith know about this? Faith!" Elle hollered for her sister. "Oh my god, are you two having an affair?"

"What's going on?" Faith rushed in the room bewildered, Mason and Ben right on her heels.

"Evan's not getting married." Elle blurted.

"What?" Shocked, Faith wiped her flour covered hands on her apron waiting for an explanation.

"It wouldn't be the first wedding she derailed." Mason's words created an awkward silence in the already tense room.

"Stop it. That was your choice. I had nothing to do with that," Serena hissed at him.

"I am marrying Claire." Evan raised his voice to be heard, then clarified, "Just not here."

"No, you can't," Faith pleaded with her brother.

"Somebody please tell me what happened? Is it the ghost?" Elle stomped the heel of her combat boot on the wood floor in frustration, then zeroed in on Mason. "And who are you? You weren't here for the party."

"You saw a ghost? We might need to talk to you, too." Ben tried to capture Elle's attention.

"Stay away from my sister. Both of them. Elle, let's go. I'll walk you to your car." Nudging Elle towards the door, he glared at Ben.

"Evan… Wait. This isn't just about you. Our business... Your wedding is important. And Claire really wants this!" Faith's voice rose in desperation.

"I won't take a chance with Claire here if Richie is hanging around. Either we're all imagining this and that makes this house dangerous, or the spirit of Richie is real and he is dangerous. He hurt her."

"But what does Claire want? Did you even talk to her about it before you came over here to bully us?" Faith's ponytail whipped back and forth with every jerk of her head.

"Wait. Richie? Isn't that the guy that died here?" Elle's voice was filled with awe.

"If it helps any, it's not really Claire he's after." Mason spoke up again.

"What are you talking about?" Evan eyed him suspiciously.

"He's angry, but he's more focused on Serena. He thinks she pushed him down the stairs, and took the money." Mason watched Evan's reaction carefully.

"That's not right." Evan's expression changed from anger to horror as he turned from Mason to Serena. She saw his inner mental workings playing out on his face and knew it wasn't a far hop to suspicion.

"I'm just telling you what I felt on the stairs last night. I didn't even know his name or what happened," Mason explained calmly.

"No." Evan ran a hand through his hair, obviously upset.

"What exactly have you been up to here, Rena?" The question was spoken calmly but all she heard was the accusation in his voice. Again.

"This is none of your business, Mason."

"I believe it is."

"Can we talk about this later?" Rolling her eyes, she motioned to the now crowded room. "This was supposed to be a private conversation."

"Well, it's over now. Come on, I think we should all go." Evan pushed at his sisters again.

"I'm not going anywhere. I've got pies to bake. I work here, remember?" Placing her floured hands on her hips, Faith planted her feet firmly on the ground.

"Jake may have something to say about that," Evan muttered.

"Jake's not a lunkheaded fool," Faith replied with a snort.

"Come on, Evan." Grabbing his arm Elle pushed him towards the foyer. After sizing Mason up one last time, Evan decided to move dragging Elle with him. Elle looked back at Faith, motioning with her spiky hair for her to follow. Ben quietly trailed behind them leaving Serena and Mason alone.

"Why are you here?" Suddenly tired, she sat in the

nearest chair.

"You know why."

"It wasn't enough that you tried to put the blame on me back then, or ruin yourself and take all of us with you?" She couldn't hide the hurt in her voice. Anger was easy, but if she let the pain out, it would cripple her.

"What? You're accusing me now? That's rich." His defensive reply was automatic. Mason closed his eyes and sighed. Taking a seat across from her, he lowered his voice. "If you needed money so badly, I would have given you everything."

"Do I look like I need money?" Sitting up straighter, she glared at him.

"No, and that just proves my point."

"Is that why you're here? Because you think I took your money?" The anger sprouted new wings.

"Rena, you know why I'm here and it has nothing to do with money."

"Yet you keep bringing it up."

"No, you keep bringing it up. Guilty conscious?" Narrowing his eyes on her, he let out a breath. "I'm still trying to piece this together. Are you working these people?"

"Get out!" Enraged, she stood. "I've changed my mind. I don't want you here."

"You need my help and I've already told you, I'm not leaving."

"I don't need you. Ben and I can do this without you."

"Ben works for me. If I go, so does he and all of the equipment." He sat nonplussed.

A stream of angry curses erupted from her mouth. She slapped a hand over it to stop it.

"I'm not leaving." With a smirk, he stood. Mason walked up to her, so close she could feel the heat from his body. Only touching her with his breath, he whispered in her ear. "We are bound."

His gold eyes burned through her, then he smiled casually.

"Tell your friends to come back tonight."

Serena watched him walk away, and fought the urge to throw something at him. Needing to work out this frustration, she headed to the big room, which she thought of as her studio. She would do what she did best. Dance. And maybe somewhere in the swirling music and emotions she would find some answers. She knew before she started the only answer she would hear was her grandmother's voice.

"Careful what you wish for, girl."

CHAPTER 5

Mason paced the upstairs landing, his restless movements finding a loose board underfoot. The timing of the floorboard creaking became more frequent with each pass. He had made it a point to stay clear of Serena, hoping to give her some time to cool off. He needed time, too. Where she was concerned he tended to let his emotions get away from him. Between his fits of restlessness, he managed to spend some of the day going over Ben's case notes. If they were accurate, this place was a goldmine.

He suppressed that thought before it could evolve into something more. No, he wouldn't send her running again. He needed to show her he could be trusted.

A small voice reminded him that he didn't fully trust her either. *Agh*. Why had he accused her like that? He had baited her on purpose. The answer was simple. He needed to know the truth. The money went missing the same time she did. He didn't care about the money, but he did care about her.

"Hey, what's up?" Ben suddenly appeared in the doorway of his room.

"Nothing. Just waiting. Are they coming?" Mason stopped before his foot landed on the loose board again. Glad to have his line of thinking derailed, he turned back towards Ben.

"I think so." Putting his hands in his pockets, Ben leaned on the door frame casually.

"Any changes?"

"Not much today." Ben paused, regarding Mason more closely then added, "We can put this off awhile."

"No. If they come, we'll do what we can. Faith may trigger something. It seems as though she's experienced most of what's going on here. We're set up for video?"

"Of course. I have monitors set up so we can watch from my room." Ben jerked his head towards the room he had been using. Several monitors and his laptop were already set up and waiting on the desk.

"Good. Just that room?"

"Yeah, for now. Why?"

"Has Serena spoken to you about the other one?" The unexpected experience earlier had given cause for concern. The voice had been unusually clear and menacing.

"Not much."

"Keep an eye out for him. He's an angry one." Mason paused, testing the air around him. "Speaking of angry, the deputy could cause some problems."

"He seems harmless enough. Just trying to look out for his family." Hands still in his pockets, Ben shrugged, his blue eyes focused on Mason.

"Do you think there's something between him and Serena?"

"God, Mason. Stop. No, nothing like that. They're friends and before you start looking at me cross-eyed, remember I'm your friend." Pushing himself from the doorframe, he stood nose to nose with Mason.

"Sorry, Ben. She makes me crazy." Turning away, Mason gripped the railing overlooking the foyer. The protective attitude the deputy had shown towards Serena had made his blood boil.

"Maybe you should go. Get back to the office, the restaurant or take a vacation."

"No." After the lengthy search, the thought of leaving her made his chest hurt.

"She's here, Mace. She's not going anywhere." Ben gave him a friendly pat on the shoulder. Mason knew his friend was trying to calm him down, but his thoughts kept nagging at him.

"I can't."

"Then you'd better chill out," Ben warned, then lowered his voice. "Do you really think she took the money?"

"I don't know." He honestly didn't. He wanted to believe she was innocent, but he knew his feelings for her could be blinding him to the truth.

"Well, I don't, and if you keep bringing it up you might lose her for good."

"What about the other thing?"

"She wouldn't have done that." The incredulous look Ben gave him made him question his own reasoning.

"Then who did? She implied it was me."

"She left because of it."

"Yeah, but what a cover. Set up that as a reason to leave, then run off with the money."

"Man, you are one suspicious son of a bitch. If all she wanted was money, all she had to do was stay with you. Instead she ran. Right now, I don't blame her." Ben turned for the stairs, but looked back over his shoulder. "Chill out, we need you level-headed."

As Mason watched his friend descend the staircase, the heavy wooden door opened letting in a humid breeze. To his surprise the younger sister with the sassy hair and attitude walked in, not Faith.

"I'm here," she called out unsurely.

"We're expecting Faith," Ben informed her as he reached the foyer.

"Elle?" Serena's voice came from the parlor. "I thought you went home."

Mason watched as Serena came forward, the sight of her so familiar his soul yearned for her.

"And miss this? Are you nuts? I'll take a sick day or something." The little snorting noise that followed reminded him of Faith.

"We don't need an audience. In fact, it's better if there's not a lot of people here." From Ben's curt reply, Mason knew he had annoyed him with his paranoia.

"Does Evan know you're here?" Her mention of the deputy riled him, but Mason could read the concern on Serena's face.

"I don't think so, but who cares?" Elle gave an eye roll accompanied by a jerk of her head. Definitely a family resemblance.

"The last thing we need is for him to show up angry. The last time..." Shaking her dark curls, Serena let the statement hang.

"Yeah, that was wild." Elle nodded in agreement, looking nervously behind her at the mirror that hung in the foyer.

"Last time what? Are you afraid of him?" Ben obviously was picking up something.

"No, not him. His temper.... They feed off of it."

The front door opened again interrupting Serena's explanation. This time Faith walked in.

"Oh, hey... Elle, I thought you left."

"Mom didn't tell you?"

"No, I haven't seen her."

"Let's hope she hasn't told Evan." Serena rolled her eyes, then asked. "Any more news on the wedding?"

"No," Faith remarked with a flip of her ponytail. "He doesn't want it here, but he's promised not to bring it up to Claire until we can find a way to clear this up."

Mason watched curiously taking in the exchange. Serena seemed calm.

"We will, but it may take some time."

"Let's do this." Elle clapped her hands together, then pumped her fists into the air. "We've got to get rid of Richie and get this wedding back on track."

"Elle... Faith never met Richie, neither have you. Faith is here about the other ghost." Serena tried to explain.

"Oh... ok." Elle gave a small pout, but shrugged it

off. "I'm game, whatever."

"It doesn't work that way..," Ben started to argue.

"Let her stay." Faith wrapped an arm around Elle's thin frame.

"Ok." Once the decision was made, Ben was all business. "Faith, we need you upstairs in the yellow room. Sit quietly and think about the times before. Maybe if we're lucky, we can figure out a trigger."

"Seems simple enough." Faith started up the stairs.

When Elle tried to follow her, Ben stepped in her way. "No, she needs to be alone."

"Well, how can I watch from down here. You can't let her go alone."

"She won't be alone," Mason spoke up finally. All heads turned up to where he stood on the landing.

"Oh."

"I have monitors set up in my room. Come on." Ben motioned for Elle to start up the stairs, then followed.

"Monitors?"

"Video equipment in case the ghost shows herself again, and so we have a record of what happens."

"Oh."

"I thought you were a DJ or something. Can't you say anything but 'oh'?" Ben smirked at her back.

"How about 'You're an asshole!'?" The diamond stud in her nose glinted with the jerky movement of her head, but she kept moving up the staircase.

"And you're not much of a conversationalist, are you? By the way, you stayed to see Gil, didn't you?"

"Shut up!" Elle whispered furiously, then glanced back at Ben. "How did you know?"

"It's a hormonal thing. I can usually sense changes. Last night you were eyeing him and..."

"Shut up!"

"Ok, ok. In here." Reaching the top of the stairs he pointed to his room.

Amused, Mason watched them settle in for the show then turned back to see Serena watching him from the foot of the stairs.

"Rena, aren't you coming up?"

"I don't think that's a good idea."

"We need you up here, and I promise to keep my distance." He gave her a devilish grin.

"Fine."

Faith was waiting outside the bedroom door biting her lip. "Now?"

"It's ok. Go on in. We'll be right here watching and listening. If you feel like it's too much for you, just step out of the room. You can leave at any time. Remember that." Serena's voice was very reassuring, as she climbed the stairs gracefully.

Faith nodded one last time and went in, leaving the door open. Mason took a deep breath and waited for Serena to join him. "Let's go in, shall we?"

"Ok. Do you feel anything?" Her dark eyes bore into his, and he felt the stirring and longing.

"That's a loaded question."

"I meant the room," she snapped, perhaps a bit harshly.

Never taking his eyes from hers he answered, "Sadness. Traces of it almost everywhere."

"Guys..." Ben motioned for them to watch the monitor.

Through the monitor they could see Faith walking around the room. Stopping in front of the window, she put a hand to the glass. Touching her head to the window, she stared out for a few minutes then began to pace again. Ben watched the meters, waiting for something to move.

"I should go in there, see if I feel anything or ask questions." Mason crossed his arms trying not to be impatient. Ben was the master of waiting and watching, he on the other hand needed to make something happen.

"No, I don't think so. She's usually alone when it happens." Serena moved closer to the screen for a better look.

"Nothing's happening now," Elle whispered loudly.

"Give it time."

"She's in this house almost every day. She has a connection. It shouldn't..."

"Mace," Ben warned.

"Sorry. I'll just go in for a minute, and tell her to ask a few questions. Is there an EVP recorder in there?"

"Here. Give her this one. It's on. Just tell her to hold still while she asks questions then wait a minute in between questions." Ben went into automatic instruction mode as he checked to make sure the recorder was working.

"Yeah, I know," Mason reminded him.

"Sorry, right."

Mason took the recorder and left the room. He hated the waiting that was involved. Normally, he just felt, and got a response. As he neared the door to the front bedroom, he called out Faith's name, not wanting to scare her.

"What?" Her cautious reply came from the open door way.

Before he reached it, the door slammed shut in his

face. Stunned, he stepped back. "Faith, did you do that?"

"No."

"It's ok. They can see you." A soft weeping sounded. "Faith?"

Before she could answer, Mason heard heavy footsteps on the stairs, moving quickly towards him. He held still waiting. A frozen breeze passed through him, stealing his breath away. The door in front of him flew open. Making eye contact with a wide eyed Faith through the opening, he tried to move forward. He felt a surge of anger, and a roaring in his head then the door slammed shut again. This time the lock clicked and the weeping grew louder. Mason reached for the door knob, and the frigid air engulfed him once again. Not being able to breathe, he fell to his knees grabbing at his chest. He thought he heard someone call his name as he slid to the floor, shivering.

"Mace. Hey man, talk to me." Ben's hands clasped on to his shoulders, and shook him gently. Mason tried to open his eyes, to move, to speak, but it was all too difficult. Another shake, this time not so gentle. His eyes rolled open a sliver, and he saw Serena's concerned face leaning over him.

"Cold..." His voice came out in a low whisper.

"Ok, hun. I'll get a blanket." Her face disappeared out of his sight, and he felt panic.

"Rena," he croaked.

⁓

Serena flew to the nearest room and ripped the blanket from the bed. This had only happened once before, when Mason was taken by surprise. She rushed back and gave the blanket to Ben. "Put this around him. I'll go make some tea."

"Faith, are you ok in there?" Elle asked through the door.

The door opened slowly. Faith emerged, fresh tears glistened on her face. "Oh, my... Is he ok?"

"He'll be fine. Ben, try to get him to his room, and I'll make tea. I think everyone could use some."

"Rena." The hoarse whisper made her jump. From under the blanket, Mason reached out a hand for her ankle.

Ben's eyes pleaded with her. "He needs you."

"I'll make tea, that'll warm him up."

"Let Elle do it." Ben looked to Elle. "You can make tea, right?"

"Yeah, I guess."

"Come on, I'll do it." Faith wiped at her face.

"Faith, you're too upset."

"No, I need something to do. Come on, Elle. Come help me."

"Take the service stairs. Just to be safe." Serena reached for Mason as Ben helped him off the floor.

"Holler if something happens," Ben added putting a shoulder under Mason's arm. Serena wrapping an arm around his waist from the opposite side, heard him gasp at her touch. They managed to get him to his room, and let him fall onto the bed.

"Nooooo," he moaned when Serena let him go.

Ben looked to her expectantly. He didn't know what he was asking. He couldn't. Being so near Mason was torture.

"Please, Rena. The sooner he recovers the sooner we can get some answers."

"You haven't listened to the audio. We may have picked something up." She tried to argue, but Ben's face was determined.

"Fine." Giving in, she lifted the blanket and climbed next to Mason cradling his head on her chest. His eyes fluttered open briefly then closed again.

"I'll check on the girls then start downloading files." Ben closed the door behind him.

Serena gazed down at him. The softness of his full lips and dark lashes made him seem so innocent. She wanted desperately to believe in him, in them. Too much had happened between them. They couldn't go back to the way things were in the beginning. Once the trust had been broken, doubt had crept in, dispelling the magic.

Mason's body convulsed with shivers, he moaned and pulled her closer.

"It's ok, hun. I'm here," she whispered wanly. "Rest. I promise I won't leave you. We'll dream together." Pulling the blanket closer around them, she noticed his skin was already warming some. She knew they'd both sleep peacefully.

The chill grayness of the room was already fading to a more comfortable warmth, but she knew behind it the tragic spirits confined here would surface again to challenge them.

Closing her eyes, she welcomed the dreams and memories she knew would come. If they weren't meant to be together in this life, they would always have the memories of their last.

CHAPTER 6

Serena woke, her body covered in sweat. Pushing at the heavy blanket encasing her, she kicked her foot to let air flow underneath. The wave of cool air only reminded her of the heat source now at her back. Mason must have shed his shirt sometime during the night. His bare skin burned into hers. Her sweat soaked shirt was trapped between them. Serena tried to roll away from him, but his arm tightened around her pulling her back.

"Don't go. Not yet."

"You're ok?"

"Yes, thank you, but I don't want to let go just yet."

The sunlight peeking through the curtain cast a hazy warm light over the bed. Between the softness of the bed and the hardness of Mason's body behind her she was also hesitant to leave.

Without turning to look at him, she asked softly, "What happened last night?"

"He was so angry."

"You shouldn't have done that Mason. You should have stayed in the room with us."

"Did I scare you, love? Worried about me?" She could hear the smile in his voice.

"Of course. I wouldn't be here otherwise. You know you should be more careful."

"Thanks for that." He planted a small kiss on her cheek. The rush of love and desire flooded through her. Having him so close was torture. "Did Ben get anything?"

"I don't know. He was going to check the EVP's when he left us."

"You didn't leave me." It wasn't a question.

"How do you know?"

"The tea's cold."

She laughed. The tea she had been so worried about sat next to the bed untouched.

"You're the best thing to warm me," he whispered seductively in her ear.

"I think we both slept soundly." Serena tried to downplay the raging emotions that only his presence could invoke. The dreams had been real and vivid leaving her feeling raw and vulnerable.

"Always with you." His simple statement had her blinking away tears.

A sharp knock at the door interrupted their moment. The door opened a crack and Ben stuck his head in. "Hey you guys up?"

"Yeah." Serena moved to sit up forcing Mason to let her go.

"You good, man?" Ben opened the door wider to see for himself.

"The only thing wrong with this picture, is you standing in my doorway."

"Yeah, right." Satisfied with Mason's sarcastic answer, Ben acknowledged his concern. "That was a bad one."

"Did you get anything?" Mason brushed it off.

"Well, the video clearly shows the door closing and opening on its own. Faith was nowhere near it."

"The EVP recorder was on?" Mason asked.

"Yeah, I turned it on when I gave it to you." Ben's eyes gleamed with excitement.

"Did you hear him?" Serena had hoped the recordings would shed some light on what needed to be done.

"Oh, yeah..."

"Hey! You guys here?" Faith's voice sounded from downstairs interrupting Ben's report.

"Up here!" Ben hollered from the doorway.

Jake entered first, focusing on Ben. "You should have waited until I was here."

"I told him everything was fine," Faith called from behind him.

"You still should have waited." Finally noticing Mason and Serena in the bed, Jake stammered, "Oh... Sorry."

"It's ok." Serena laughed at Jake's flustered expression. Then hoping to calm him, she suggested, "Let's go downstairs and make coffee."

"You're ok?" Faith asked Mason as she squeezed

by Jake.

"Yes, I'm fine. Sometimes when they get too close it drains me. He walked through me twice last night."

"Wait..." Ben pushed Jake out of his way and ran out of the room. He returned with a recorder in his hand. Pushing a button, he began to speak. "This is Mason Del Toro's account of his experience on..."

"Do we have to do this now?" Mason agitated, reached for Serena's hand absently. She welcomed its warmth, wishing things could always be that simple between them.

"Yes, first account. It's important. I'd like to see if it matches the EVP, and Faith's account." Ben motioned for him to continue.

"Ok, fine. This is Mason Del Toro, yada yada. We were watching the monitor from Ben's room. I decided to bring the EVP recorder into the front bedroom where Faith was, to ask questions. It didn't seem like anything was happening." He stopped suddenly, using his free hand to point at Faith. "Should she be here?"

"It's ok. I got her statement last night before she left."

Mason nodded and continued, "When I neared the doorway I called out. I didn't want to frighten her. The door slammed in my face. Then I heard footsteps coming up the stairs. I stayed still hoping the EVP was picking it up. Then I felt the cold. It was like someone had opened a freezer door. It took my breath away. The door flew open. I saw Faith in the room. She looked frightened. I meant to go to her, but the door slammed shut again, and I heard the lock click. There was so much anger, violence. It was a red haze. Then the cold again, I couldn't breathe. I don't remember much else." He looked into Serena's eyes. "Except Rena."

"Ok, great." Ben snapped off the recorder. "Now coffee.... And maybe some breakfast?" He gave Faith a hopeful look.

"Ok," Faith laughed, "Come on, Jake, you can help me. You, too, Ben. You can explain some of this while I cook."

"Sure." Ben happily followed them out of the room.

"Yeah, I need a shower." Letting go of his hand, Serena rose from the bed.

"Sounds great."

"Alone," she said glancing back over her shoulder. She caught him gazing hungrily at her body.

He looked up catching her eye, "I have my memories. They'll do for now." His husky voice floated across the room to her.

Serena turned and closed the bedroom door without looking back at him. She had those same memories too and no amount of magic could erase them.

⁀◦⁀

"Jake, I'll be fine. They can't control when it happens." Faith's voice reached Serena before she entered the kitchen.

"What about last night?" Obviously Jake was still upset. Serena hurried in hoping to diffuse any argument.

"That's the first time in months anything has happened, and it was in that room. I normally don't go upstairs at all. When I'm here, I'm in the kitchen."

"Really?" Ben asked from his favorite chair at the island counter.

"One night you were in here. Remember?" Jake reminded Faith of the night she had first heard the music.

"Ok you two." Serena tried to calm them.

"You know... You know what it does to her. I don't like it." Jake turned on her, pointing a finger in her direction.

"Jake, you know it can't hurt y'all. It's like a video replaying a memory over and over, that's all."

"That's all? It didn't feel like a video to me." Jake paced towards the back door.

"I've got to help her find the baby. That's what she wants. I know it," Faith spoke up from her post at the stove.

"Why you?" Mason's voice came unexpectedly from behind Serena making her jump. Walking straight up to Faith, he gazed into her eyes. "Why do you think she picked you and not Serena?"

Serena gasped at hearing the question she had been asking herself since the first episode.

"The baby. She knows." Faith placed a hand on her stomach.

"Knows what?" Mason's eyes narrowed on Faith.

"Jake and I had a lot in common with them." Faith's dark eyes darted nervously from Mason to Jake guiltily.

"Oh, just tell them, babe. If it'll help end this." Hand on hips, Jake hung his head with a sigh.

Serena pushed Mason out of her way to get to Faith. "Oh, hun. You were pregnant back then..." She hugged her friend tightly. "Why didn't you say? I just thought it was because you are a mother, too."

"Well, I thought I was, but I wasn't. Jake didn't know. Nobody did."

"Kids?" Mason turned to Jake. "Yours?"

"No, she was married to someone else." Jake's jaw clenched tightly as he turned away.

"Ah..." Taking in the new information, Mason's gaze wandered back to Faith.

"So she wants you to help find the baby like it's lost, but she should know where it is," Ben reasoned.

"I thought maybe it died. She's so sad. It's unbearable." Faith still leaning on Serena, looked to Mason for confirmation.

Mason nodded in agreement.

Turning back towards them, Jake pulled at the collar of his shirt. "I've got to get to work. I can't eat anyway. I don't like Faith here without me. And I don't want to be here either."

"I'm not sure that's wise." Mason was now focused on Jake, watching him intently.

"What?"

"You're connected too. Last night I felt him."

"Him?" Hooking a finger in the neckband of his undershirt, Jake pulled and twisted the thin material away from himself.

"Yes, what we are assuming is the father. He is angry, and violent. Still."

"I thought it was a video. Videos can't hurt you," Jake mimicked Serena's words.

"It's not wise for Evan to be here either," Serena cautioned, "He used his anger once. It could happen again."

"Nah, we're good now. That's over." His finger still hanging on his neckband, Jake shrugged.

"Why do you keep pulling at your shirt?" Mason asked.

"I gotta go." Jake looked down at his shirt, dropping his hand quickly.

"Wait. What are you feeling right now?"

"Can't breathe. Uncomfortable." Jake shrugged again. "I've felt it before, like somebody's watching me. I gotta go."

Not bothering to walk through the house again, Jake exited through the back door. Faith ran after him, ponytail bouncing wildly.

Stunned, they stood for a moment taking in the information. Mason broke the silence first. "Amazing."

"This is a powder keg," Serena whispered loudly realizing the connections and ties went deeper than she imagined.

"So do we keep them apart, or do we get them all together and set it off?" Ben wondered out loud.

"No. You can't guarantee the outcome. They are my friends, my family." She had been so careful to keep this from them all. Now she had to figure a way out without losing their friendship.

"Serena, that's the point." Ben's tone was sharp as he struggled to make her understand. "They are your friends. They are family. Makes it harder to control emotions. You're planning a wedding here. They will all be here together eventually. Do you want it to go off at the wedding, or before?"

"No, there's got to be a better way." Serena shook her head, then added a warning to them both. "And this stays here. You won't use them."

"This is real, Rena. We have proof." Ben's argument took him from his chair. Standing, he leaned on the counter.

"No. No TV."

"No TV," Mason agreed. "I'm done with that. It was Sebastian and Eva's idea, never mine."

The mention of his ex-fiancé's name sent a surge of jealousy through her. She tried to wipe it from her mind before he could read her.

"When I ended it, it was over," he said simply, his gold eyes boring into hers.

"I know. I am surprised you didn't go back to her when I left. I got the feeling it wasn't over for her." Serena couldn't help the snarky remark.

"I was too busy trying to find you." His eyes never left hers.

"Hey, let's talk about now." Ben raised his eyebrows at them. "What's the game plan?"

"Give them a few days." Turning her attention back to Ben and the present, she caught a whiff of over-cooked eggs.

"But..."

"No, I mean it. Leave them alone and give me time to figure out how to help them separately."

"What about the other girl?" Ben suggested.

"No, Evan will do his best to keep Claire away. I wouldn't provoke him, and he needs to stay away." She turned off the stove and stirred the eggs that Faith had forgotten in her hurry to follow Jake.

"Besides it's not her Richie wants to hurt," Mason reminded them. There it was. The jab she'd been waiting for.

"Exactly. Someone else who thinks I stole their money." Picking the pan up, she was tempted to throw it at him. Instead, she turned from the stove to meet Mason's gaze over the steaming eggs.

"We can talk about that later, ok guys?" Ben's conciliatory tone broke their glaring contest.

"I thought you wanted a game plan?" Serena scraped the scrambled eggs onto a platter in front of Ben.

"Yeah, got it. We give them time. In the meantime, I'll continue to take readings and maybe we can try some more EVP stuff. Just us," he added quickly, when Serena's eyebrow lifted. Ben gave his best innocent look. "Can we eat now?"

CHAPTER 7

The house was quiet. Serena loved it when everything was at peace. Over the past few days, Mason and Ben had made it a point to stay out of her way. She paced in the dark, feeling the space around her. The walls stood strong, the air felt a bit thick and musty. She didn't mind. She lit incense and sat in the parlor watching its smoldering ember.

Her life hadn't been ideal, but whose? Realizing early, she hadn't given birth to a normal child, her mother had downplayed Serena's instincts, crediting them to a child's overactive imagination. When she didn't grow out of it, things became awkward. Thankfully her grandmother had not only understood, but encouraged her to talk of such things.

Being around other people became uncomfortable. Knowing things she shouldn't made her standout. Reading people made it hard to have close friends. Her early years were spent mostly with her grandmother, shying away from group activities. She participated only in those her mother seemed more excited about than she was. Her first formal dance was pleasant but uneventful. Her first kiss she remembered fondly. The young man was sincere at the time, but she knew it wouldn't last. Becoming comfortable with small town life, even labeled as the weird girl, she thought she could live that way forever. Her grandmother had insisted that life was not for her. She told her to live, not hide away. *"Follow where your dreams lead you."*

Her dreams, even back then, brought her to Coeur du Bayou. Dreams of walking through these rooms, feeling the wood floor beneath her feet, waiting and watching through the upstairs window, had haunted her for years. When she was finally old enough to venture out, she was drawn to historical places.

Serena's first trip to New Orleans was a disaster. The moment her feet touched the pavement in Jackson Square she was bombarded with memories. From one extreme to the other: love, pain, anger, lust. The flashes of emotions were unrelenting. Within a few hours of wandering the French Quarter, she was drained. Her acquaintances had assumed she was drunk and brought her back to the hotel where she spent the rest of the trip recovering.

The experience had taught her not to let it in all at once, but to focus and filter. Once she felt she had control, she went off in search of those old places filled with memories. Somehow she thought they were the key to finding whatever it was she was searching for. She didn't even know at the time. There was a longing in her soul that kept her searching for the magic. It was like a quest for knowledge. The unending trail of breadcrumbs that would lead to the elusive meaning of life. It led her down the path of spirituality.

For her, the relationship between music and movement was a sacred dance. Dance became her passion and her release. That dance ultimately lead to Mason. Working with a small troupe of belly dancers performing along the coast, the fateful dance had occurred at a restaurant owned by Mason's family.

The smoke from the incense danced before her as she remembered the jolt of recognition. Looking across the audience into his fierce gaze, her step had faltered. Her rhythm broken, she was transported into another time. The memory so clear. His skin, slick from perspiration, unyielding against hers. His mouth hot with desire leaving a trail of kisses down her stomach. His eyes, glowing in the firelight, as he looked up at her. His voice, smooth as silk. "You are mine. We are bound forever."

Fighting to recover the dance, she had finished as gracefully as possible. Searching for him in the crowd, she thought maybe she was mistaken and had dreamed the whole thing. If he had been there, maybe he hadn't felt what she had. Disappointed, she gave up and went home.

Two days later, there he was waiting on the beach, where she had cast the spell and wished for him. At first she thought maybe it was just a coincidence, then he spoke.

"I came back for you."

It had to be magic. It was magic. He was like her. Their attraction was undeniable and their passion for each other burned so hot it overwhelmed her. The first time they made love she was swept away to a different time on a wave of sensation like nothing she had ever experienced before.

Assuming her search was over, she happily helped him scout locations for his new venture, Spirit Catchers, Inc. He wanted her to be a member of their team and follow him to home base, which to her surprise meant back to Louisiana. All of the coincidences compelled her to believe in the magic. It wasn't until their arrival home that she learned he had ended his engagement with his fiancé Eva the night he saw her dance. To her, it was further proof they were meant to be.

"Rena?" His voice came from the foyer, slipping through the darkness and pulling her back to the present.

"I told you to use the service stairs." Not bothering to hide her concern.

"I did." Mason looked around anxiously. "I smell smoke."

"It's just incense."

"No, I get whiffs of smoke every now and then since the other night."

"Did you tell Ben?" Sniffing the air around her, all she caught was the musky scent of Mason and the incense.

"Yeah, I mean not just now, but before, yes." He ran a hand through his dark hair, pushing it from his forehead.

"He'll want to know." Her voice sounded small and sad, even to her.

"Are you ok?"

"Huh? Oh, yes, I'm fine."

"I'm here if you need to talk."

"I'm well aware that you are here." She sighed heavily.

He crossed the room in darkness, and sat next to her. "We need to clear this up."

"Mason, it's not a matter of saying words, you know that."

"Mi Amor." Reaching for her hand, he brought it softly to his face. "I'm here, love. I came back for you, remember?"

Letting herself remember, she caressed his face. The heat was instant, a flame of desire spread through her. Drawn like a magnet, her body turned instinctively towards him. The kiss was more than physical, it was magic. Their souls intertwined and rejoiced. Floating with the emotion, she let go, and let the feeling take over. Time slipped away.

Serena felt the house shift beneath her abruptly, jolting her back into her surroundings.

Mason felt when she pulled away and groaned. "No, no, no."

"Mason, stop."

Every part of his body was on fire for her. He gazed up at her through heavy lidded eyes. Not willing to let her go he caressed her thighs that straddled him. "Come back," he purred.

"Mason," she hissed, slapping at his hands and

pulling at her skirt that was now bunched around her waist. "Did you feel that?"

"Always with you. All I can do is feel. You're like a drug to me." His hand traveled up her leg again.

"No, the house." Serena grabbed his wrist and held it still.

He immediately stilled, listening carefully to the darkness. Not sensing anything, he asked, "What did you feel?"

"The house. I can feel it sometimes. It's hard to explain."

"I think I'm jealous, if it can distract you from me so easily." Teasingly, he bucked his hips suggestively under her.

Ben cleared his throat from the foyer. "Guys? Ummm, hate to interrupt, but did something just happen?"

"Reuben, you are fast becoming my least favorite person on the planet." Mason dropped his arms heavily on the sofa.

Serena gave him one last heated look, then climbed off of him. He heard movement then the soft glow of a candle surrounded them.

"What's going on Ben?" she asked worriedly.

"Readings just spiked."

"Where?"

"Everywhere, it seemed."

"I don't know. It felt different." Serena turned back to him. "Mason, did you..."

"I didn't feel anything." Aggravated he ran a hand through his hair. "Not the house, anyway."

"The time?" Serena considered as she asked Ben.

"I got it. It just seemed like something had to be happening. I didn't hear anything up there, so I thought it was down here."

"Something was happening down here, but it didn't concern you." Mason sat up throwing a pillow from the sofa at Ben.

"Yeah.... Ok." Catching it, Ben rolled his eyes at Mason. "I don't think you set off an EMF, Casanova."

He gave Ben a smirk. "You'd be surprised."

"Cut it out." Serena grabbed the pillow from Ben and placed it back on the sofa. Sweeping her eyes over them, the gravity of moment stilled them and drew their attention. "The house. It's not like before. It thinks it was trying to get my attention."

"There's no door slamming... No crying." Ben listened, turning towards the foyer, meter in hand.

"Serena, you are definitely connected to this house." Hearing the uncertainty in Serena's voice pained him. Wanting to reassure her, Mason got up from the sofa to hug her.

"But why can't I see it." The desperation in Serena's voice had him pacing trying to sense any activity.

"Stay off the stairs."

He turned back to her smiling. "Yes, dear."

"It's not her. I don't feel her, but I don't want to take the chance of him walking through you again."

"I'll be more careful, I promise," he admitted, walking back to her and planting a kiss on her forehead. "To be honest, I wasn't expecting anything like that. It caught me off guard."

"No shit," Ben muttered under his breath.

Mason stepped away from Serena, formulating a sarcastic answer to Ben's remark. His comeback was silenced by his vision suddenly wavering before him.

The beeping meter sounded far away. Gasping, he put a hand out in front of him. The hand held a fist full of money. Not his hand. The room was familiar, the same room he was in, but he was seeing through someone else's eyes. A sound caught his attention. Serena's friend with the big blue eyes stood shivering in some kind of costume, her bruised face terrified. Something moved in his peripheral vision. He caught a glimpse of familiar bare feet before a splitting pain erupted in his skull. He went down, wood splintering beneath him.

Mason cried out falling to his hands and knees.

"Mace, what's wrong?" Ben asked quietly.

He looked from Ben's anxious face to Serena's worried one.

"Rena... It was you."

"What are you talking about?"

"He showed me. The money.... The other girl... You." Putting his hand over his face, he groaned. "Did you kill him?"

"Mason, dude." Ben's warning came too late.

"No, I didn't," she hissed. "The more important question is, why are you so quick to accuse me? Without trust there's nothing for us."

"He showed me." Getting to his feet slowly, he shook his head again to clear the vision from his mind.

"I don't care."

"Rena, wait." He reached for her. She pushed him away.

"No! He came into my house, threatening me. He hurt my friend, and I wasn't about to let him do it again." Her voice rose as the anger rolled off of her in waves. "He's lucky I didn't kill him."

"Hey… Ummm. Let's calm down, and…" Ben tried to step between them.

Serena's glare stopped his suggestion cold. With a swish of her skirt, she wove her way between them and left the room.

The meter in Ben's hand sounded harshly again. Movement from the mantel caught their attention. A candlestick wobbled as if bumped by an unseen hand. It teetered close to the edge, rocking back and forth on its base, until finally working its way over the side. It crashed to the floor, and rolled on its side, finally coming to rest at Mason's feet.

CHAPTER 8

Mason had no trouble finding the diner. Cypress Point was not by any means a large town. After a slight hesitation, he had planned a meeting with Faith and Jake. Not one for waiting idly by, he felt he needed to do something. The house and Serena had been oddly quiet. She came and went without so much as a glance in his direction. He gave her space, not wanting to push. He couldn't blame her really. Her question had stumped him, but it did need an answer.

Why was he so ready to accuse her of stealing? Of murder? Good god. He gripped the steering wheel with both hands, grimacing. The hurt on her face had pained him greatly. The anger, however, had frightened him a little. There was no doubt in his mind he loved her. He felt it with every fiber of his body and soul. Obviously, there were other issues yet to be uncovered.

In an attempt to help move things along, he set up the meeting with Faith and Jake away from the house. Questioning himself on whether or not he should have consulted Serena first, he shrugged off yet another wave of self-doubt and slammed the car door. Another mistake, he was sure. Stepping onto the sidewalk, he let his gaze travel across the quaint downtown area.

Cypress Point lounged casually in a picturesque grid of neat street-work before him. A closer look revealed subtle signs of decades of economic boom and bust. There were a handful of empty commercial buildings and the rough edged main street had more than its share of tar-sealed stress cracks and potholes. The summer heat had most people indoors.

The bell over the door jingled as he entered the diner. All eyes watched him curiously. Always the outsider, he smiled. A few heads nodded in acknowledgement, others looked away.

"Mason, over here," Faith called out from a booth.

Questioningly, he gave a nod to the apron covering her clothes. "I thought we were going to talk."

"Yeah, come sit. Can I get you anything first?"

"No, I'm fine." Mason slid into the booth across from Jake who eyed him warily.

"What do you want?" Not bothering with a greeting, Jake obviously wanted to get straight to the point. From the thin layer of dust covering his clothes, Mason assumed he had come from work. By his attitude, he assumed Jake intended to return to his fields after their meeting.

"Jake," Faith chided slipping into the seat next to him.

"Look, I understand this is weird for both of you. Serena is worried about everyone being at the house together. So I'm proposing a way to find out what happened there without involving everyone at the same time."

"What do you mean?" Faith's expression was curious as she leaned forward on the table.

"Hypnosis." It was the only solution he had been able to come up with. Waiting for the ghost was unreasonable. He could control the sessions and hopefully get to the bottom of it quickly.

"What?" Jake's surprised reaction was a welcome, but short lived change from the rank suspicion he had been sending Mason's way.

"Sometimes, a past life regression is helpful in shedding light on current haunting events and why they are happening." Mason tried to explain his reasoning for the suggestion. He knew most people would never consider voluntarily submitting themselves to hypnosis.

"Who would do it?" Faith asked sitting up a little straighter, biting on her lip.

"Me."

"I don't know." Placing his rough hands on the table in front of him, Jake shook his head unsurely.

"The female presence in the house has shown you pieces of her life already. You think she's looking for her child, but it's not clear. This may help." Mason directed his argument to Faith.

Faith swallowed hard then nodded her head slowly.

"Can I be there?" Jake ran a hand through his hair. His request was a reluctant acceptance of Faith's decision.

"I don't think that's a good idea considering your connection, but if you're willing we could do a session with you, too. Separately of course."

"No way." Jake's raised voice caused a few heads to turn their way.

Faith took Jake's hand, and whispered, "Look, we have to figure this out. Coeur du Bayou is important, not just to me, but Serena, too. If you think it'll help, I'll do it."

When Jake started to protest, she squeezed his hand. "Jake, it'll be fine."

"Ben and Serena will be present, to record and witness."

"Witness?" Jake's eyes narrowed on him.

"Just to verify. It's good to have more than one account."

"I don't like it, but I want this to be over." Looking down at their hands on the table, Jake shook his head again.

"Ok, I'd suggest we keep this private. No offense, but it's better without an audience. Too many distractions."

Faith gave him a puzzled look.

"Your sister?"

"Oh, no, Elle had to go back home. And Claire is busy with the end of school this week."

"I should go, and leave you two to talk this over." Mason sat up preparing to leave the booth.

"I said I'd do it."

"Ahh." Mason took in Faith's determined expression, and Jake's concern. Covering their entwined hands with his, he tried to reassure them both. "Serena was very clear about one thing. All of you are very dear to her, and no one will be hurt. That's why I asked both of you here together. Nothing should come between you. Not even this."

"And you and Serena?"

Pulling his hand back, he smiled at Faith sadly. "She never mentioned me, did she?"

"No."

"Well, to answer your question, not even time has been able to keep us apart." He slid from the booth, then looked back at them. "Let me know. You know where to find me."

Putting his shades on, he headed back out into the bright sunshine. He knew everyone was watching the stranger. Another side effect of being so sensitive. Being different hadn't been as rough on him as it had been for Serena. He assumed it had to do with the money. Coming from a large family that owned a chain of restaurants, people had treated him differently. He had stopped caring what other people thought of him at an early age. It simply didn't matter. Everything around him seemed to be infused with vibrations that no one else could see or feel. He loved being different; special.

His father had been a busy, distant man, and was never around much to notice Mason's sensitivities. His mother, on the other hand, encouraged him to discuss and explore his experiences. His brothers, of course, ragged him about it endlessly. Being natural skeptics, they believed it was a middle child ploy for attention.

When he had decided to use his gifts to form a team, his older brother, Gabriel had jumped at the chance to prove him wrong. Joining the team, as the skeptic, he used logic and reason to balance things out. Reuben, although not related, had come aboard with his technical expertise, being a photographer, but it soon became apparent he had abilities of his own. When emotions were running high and getting out of hand, he had a knack for easing the tension with a joke or clever change of focus. His love of research and meticulous record keeping were invaluable to the team. His younger twin brothers were as different as night and day. Thaddeus, the older twin, was quiet and awkward while Sebastian, always the wild one, had a flare for drama, trouble and women. Even so, he had leapt at the chance to experience anything supernatural, while Thad had shied away from the project.

Mason thought his team was exceptional, but had no ambition other than helping people get to the bottom of their hauntings. Eva, on the other hand, had enough ambition for them all. Not content to sit through long nights of watching and waiting, she focused on building their name and their fame. Developing and producing their own paranormal investigation TV show had been her idea, but Sebastian's need for notoriety instantly kicked in. He quickly followed her lead.

Driving slowly through the town, he admired the lake front. People here seemed friendly enough. He received a few waves, and some double takes from townsfolk who didn't recognize him. He would have never pictured Serena settling here. Seeing her near the water was natural to him, he had just assumed it would be on a beach somewhere. Images of them in the sand came instantly to mind.

The music from the radio floated through the air, changing the image in his mind's eye to a vision of Faith and Jake sitting on a blanket. Jake was singing and playing the guitar. Curious, he waited for the song to end hoping the announcer would identify it. The song ended and another began.

He drove back to Coeur du Bayou wondering what it meant. Coeur du Bayou. He still had trouble considering this Serena's home. It wasn't where he pictured them spending the rest of their lives. Of course, when she bought it, she hadn't considered him at all.

Jealous of a house. He was joking the first time he said it, but he was jealous. Serena had dreamed of this house long before she found it. He had dreamed of her his whole life. Mason knew he should be glad it was a house she had ran away to and not another man. He wouldn't have been able to bear that.

He drove up the long driveway to the object of his envy. There it stood. Taking a good look at it in the bright light of day, it became obvious Serena had taken great care to restore it and bring it back to life. He sucked in a breath as his thought registered. She was the magic that had brought it back to life.

CHAPTER 9

Serena stormed up the steps to her house. It was hers. This place didn't have anything to do with Mason. She finally had found a place to belong. After years of searching, this place had welcomed her and gave her peace. Even now she could feel its warmth and pull.

Ben opened the front door greeting her with a boyish grin. "Hey, there you are."

"Stop it, Ben."

"What?" Shrugging innocently, he held the door open for her.

"I won't be manipulated." Not stopping to argue, she headed for the stairs.

Her heart beating loudly, Serena climbed the stairs. With every step she was aware of the blood pumping through her veins. The building pressure causing her pulse to quicken.

The door to Mason's room gave a little creak as Serena opened it without bothering to knock. He sat on the bed with files splayed around him. His round framed glasses were oddly out of place on him, causing her to pause. The pause gave her a chance to notice how well the glasses fit with his new shorter hairstyle. The wild mane and rock star image had been replaced with an intelligent look, that made him even sexier.

"I know it's your house," Mason looked up from the file as he spoke, "but if you're planning to rent out the rooms you can't be walking in on your guests."

His first statement made her gasp. Serena wondered if he had read her thoughts somehow. Pointing out her unprofessionalism flared her anger to new heights.

"What are you up to?"

"Looking over these files." Slipping off the glasses, he motioned with them to the files on the bed next to him.

"You know what I mean. You talked to Faith and Jake without talking to me about it first." Hands on hips, she glared at him.

"I wasn't aware that was a requirement," he said simply.

"She called to tell me she was ready for her session. Were you even going to tell me about it?"

"Yes, of course. Please calm down."

Her eyes closed involuntarily as another wave of anger rolled over her.

"Rena, please. I want to apologize."

Her eyes opened at the unexpected request, and she narrowed them on him. "For?"

"Everything. Mostly my attitude and not thinking clearly. I was so happy to find you at last, I barely looked at the files or considered what you've been dealing with here. The connections."

His apology took some of the anger away. Before she could find the words to respond, he continued, "You wanted a way to find out more without setting off the powder keg. I suggested hypnosis to Faith and Jake. Separately. I wanted to talk to you first, but you seemed to need some space. Away from me. I was going to tell you once they decided, so we could discuss the best way to handle it."

Not used to seeing the rational side of him, she bit her lip considering what he proposed. Sitting on the edge of his bed, she asked, "Do you think it will work?"

"It can't hurt. If we wait for the ghost, it might take years to get answers, if at all."

Her sigh, deep from within, released the anger, but left an opening for doubt. "I don't have years."

"Ah, love, we have all the time we need."

Smiling at him wistfully, she knew he wasn't speaking of just the ghost. "So, what's the plan?"

Ben appeared suddenly in the doorway. "I vote for pizza."

"You and your stomach." Serena laughed at him.

"I swear I'm going to hang a bell on him." Mason closed his eyes in frustration. "Always interrupting."

"Whatever guys. I'll go get the pizza. You guys take all of this downstairs and we can go over it while we eat."

By the time Ben got back with the pizza, they had brought everything down to the kitchen. Serena knew they'd be more comfortable in the parlor, but was relieved when Mason didn't suggest it. Richie had been quiet after that last scene, but they didn't need a repeat.

"Reuben has pointed out some triggers," Mason began as he pulled out a stool for Serena.

"Triggers?" Serving the pizza, she passed the first loaded plate to Ben.

"Smells. Sounds." Ben took his first bite before his plate hit the counter. Inhaling deeply as he chewed.

"The gardenias. The music," Mason clarified as he accepted the next plate from Serena.

"But those things didn't make the experiences happen. They were a part of it." She waved the server in the air as she questioned their reasoning.

"Exactly." Ben managed the word between bites. His eyes focused on the steaming slices before him.

"Right," Mason agreed, his plate still untouched. At Serena's frown of confusion, he continued, "What we mean is, we can try to use them to trigger her memory, since they obviously mean something to her."

"We all smelled the gardenias. It's what led us to the sign. We've smelled it several times since then. Even Claire said she smelled it in the graveyard," she thought out loud, finally placing a slice on her plate.

"You'll have to show me where it is." Ben perked up at the mention of the graveyard.

"Nothing's really happened there." Serena thought back. Everything seemed to be contained to the house as far as she knew.

"You just said she smelled it there." Slice in midair, Ben stopped to look at her.

"Oh, yeah, but she had hit her head pretty hard. I don't know."

"Well, I want to look out there anyway. Those rubbings you sent me weren't helpful. I'm thinking maybe pictures, digitally enhanced. Who knows?" Ben wiped at his chin and shrugged.

"So we find gardenia oil for the session and see what she can remember." Mason brought them back to the subject at hand.

Serena nodded silently at Mason.

"What's wrong?"

"I wouldn't have thought of that. I should have seen. I should know." The doubt flooded through her. Staring at her plate, she began to second guess herself, considerations playing across her normally placid face.

"Rena, you wrote everything down. Without it, we'd be nowhere. You knew enough to keep the brother away. It's obviously some sort of transference, him and the father figure. You put that together." Ben offered as he waved a fresh slice at her.

"I just feel like I should know."

"I think you're too close. Too close to them, the house. Speaking of which, has no one ever mentioned smelling something burning?" Wrinkling his nose as if he conjured the smell with his words, Mason flipped through her notebook.

"No."

"Any evidence of fire?"

"No. I think the realtor would have mentioned it. I saw no evidence of a fire during the remodel." Lifting her pizza, she answered him, then put it back on her plate. Something wasn't right. Why didn't she smell what he was smelling? Why didn't the ghost come to her?

"Hmmm." Mason looked thoughtfully down at his pizza and finally began to eat.

"What I don't understand is why it's still happening? I thought the night everything came together... The fight.... I thought that would be the end of it. Nothing happened for weeks."

"But that's when you called me, right?" Ben prompted.

"Yeah, I had a feeling something bad was going to happen. I was worried about having them all here together."

"What aren't you saying?" Mason leaned forward unto the counter, his gold eyes watching her intently.

"I thought it was Richie, but at first I wasn't sure." She shrugged at him. Her first inkling that something wasn't right, was subtle, but meaningful. The damn candlestick kept moving. Just a few inches at first, breaking the symmetry of her mantle display. Thinking maybe she had moved it while dusting, she dismissed the incident. After the second time, she started watching for it. The day it had seemed to jump off the mantle in front of her, she had called Ben.

"Hello?" a cheery voice called from the foyer. Before anyone could move, Claire entered the kitchen with an armful of catalogs. "Hey, you are home! Faith must have been confused. She said you weren't back from..." Claire paused then shrugged with a laugh, "wherever you go."

Ben stood nervously, napkin in hand.

"Oh, hey you're back, too! With the pictures? Oh my god, I'm so excited. I can't wait to see them." Claire's blue eyes sparkled as she wiggled a few steps.

"Back? Pictures?" Ben crumpled his napkin in a fist, then looked to Serena gulping loudly. "Rena, help."

"Claire, come and sit. We haven't seen you in weeks." Laughing at Ben's guilty expression, Serena stood to greet her friend.

"Yeah, end of school is crazy and Evan said you had to go on a trip. Faith brought me these to look at, and I wanted to see what you thought." Claire wandered over to the end of the counter to find a clear spot to put the catalogs down.

"Oh. Good. Would you like some pizza?" Serena closed a few of the folders that were open then offered Claire her seat.

"No, I ate with Evan before he left for work."

"So he doesn't know you're here?" Serena glanced at Mason and Ben.

"No. Why? What's going on?" Finally noticing the folders, Claire leaned over to get a better look.

"Hun, why don't you just leave those here for me to look at and tomorrow I can meet you in town to talk about it?" Serena took her arm to guide Claire away from the counter and pointed her towards the door.

"Oh…" Claire blinked in surprise then gave a pout. "Well, can I at least see the pictures while I'm here?"

"Pictures?" Serena asked.

"I assume you came back to bring the pictures

from the party, right?" Claire turned back to Ben.

"Right. I think I have them upstairs...." He shifted from one foot to the other and motioned at the ceiling.

Mason laughed at Ben's expression. "Ben, stop. He's been here since the party, so have I. Surprisingly enough, Serena has even resisted the urge to leave."

"Mason." Serena hissed his name then turning to Claire she took a deep breath. "Claire, I don't know how to say this, but Evan will not be happy that you're here."

"Why?"

"He's just worried about you. Calm down."

"I am. I just don't understand why he would lie. Faith, too." Her cheeks now red, her gaze fell to the floor.

"Evan didn't want you here, so I'm sure Faith is just trying to keep the peace." Serena gave her arm a pat and moved her another step towards the door.

"He told you he didn't want me here. When?" Claire pulled away from Serena.

"The morning after the party." Mason supplied the answer.

"Oh, no. He came here?" Covering her mouth with her hands, Claire glanced around the room, her eyes watering.

"The last thing we want is to cause trouble." Ben finally finding his voice, spoke up.

"What about what I want?"

"I think you should go talk to Evan." Serena knew her friend was upset, but it would serve no purpose for them to argue about who was right or wrong.

"Preferably somewhere else." Looking down at

the half eaten slice of pizza on his plate, Ben cleared his throat nervously.

"You don't want me here either?" Claire asked Serena in a small voice.

"You are always welcome here. It's just right now with the way things are, if Evan shows up angry... You remember what happened last time."

"Yeah, that was crazy." Claire wiped at her eyes and sighed. "Do you think it'll happen again?"

"Serena is trying to prevent anyone from getting hurt." Trying to reassure her, Mason smiled at Claire.

"Evan's not like that." Quick to defend him, Claire stood straighter.

"I know Claire." Serena wrapped an arm around Claire and squeezed her shoulders. "His temper is what I'm trying to avoid."

"I thought it was over. Is this about Richie? Is this my fault?" Claire hugged her purse to her.

"No, of course not. You can't help what happened to Richie." Sending Mason a glare, she added, "It was an accident."

Mason taking her hint, nodded in agreement. "We think the ghost lady is looking for her baby. So we'll be working with Faith to figure it out."

"Oh, so you're not a photographer?" Claire asked Ben, her disappointment evident.

"Yes, I am." Ben smiled happily, and stuffed the last bite of pizza into his mouth.

"Whew. So I do have pictures somewhere of the engagement party?" She asked looking nervously from Ben to Serena with hopeful eyes.

"Yes. I'll have them edited and printed for you in a few days. Absolutely." Talking with his mouth full, Ben nodded vigorously.

The smile she gave him was brilliant, but it didn't last long. "Wait, so you all work together?"

"They didn't tell you anything, did they?" Serena squeezed her shoulders again waiting for the rapid fire questions to start.

"I guess I know who I can trust with my secrets." Eyebrows raised, Mason reopened a file.

"I wouldn't have thought Elle could help herself," Ben remarked eyeing the untouched pizza on Serena's plate.

"Elle? She knew too?"

"Sorry," Ben muttered.

"What else did I miss?" Claire looked to Serena, her expression filled with hurt. "Friends aren't supposed to keep secrets."

"I think you should talk to Evan, hun."

Fleetwood Mac suddenly blared from Claire's purse. Serena winced at the timing and felt sorry for Evan.

"Oh, I will. You can bet on that." Digging in her purse, Claire pulled out her phone and spun on her heel, heading out the door.

CHAPTER 10

The candles were lit. Even though they weren't necessary, the soft lighting helped to relax the atmosphere. In place of incense, Serena had found gardenia scented oil. It floated lightly in the air of the pale yellow room. Mason had his doubts about using this room. It was definitely the female's bedroom from the accounts of earlier activity. And his close encounter with the angry father spirit was still fresh in his mind. The alternative was the parlor and he didn't want to be interrupted by Richie again.

He told Faith to wear comfortable clothes and come alone. Not having any objections from Jake made him feel easier about the whole thing. He fully expected for Evan to show up in protest, but maybe Claire's talk had kept him away.

Faith sat on the edge of the bed in the pretty yellow room fidgeting with her ponytail.

"Relax." Mason smiled at Faith. He could feel her nervous energy.

"Easier said than done. What if it doesn't work?"

"Stop worrying about it. It won't work if you don't relax. Lie down," Ben instructed from his makeshift control area in a corner of the room. Sitting behind a small table, he adjusted the video camera on Faith. Serena lingered in the doorway, her dark eyes watching with concern.

Laying back on the pillow, Faith took a deep breath.

"Ben, are you ready?" Mason could feel the anticipation from them all. They needed to get started.

"Yeah, all set."

"Rena, please close the door. Everybody relax. Get comfortable. Faith, close your eyes and concentrate on your breathing."

They all sat in silence waiting for the room to settle. Mason keeping his voice soft, began the induction, giving Faith instructions, relaxing her with the sound of his voice.

"Remember this room. This is your room and you feel safe here. Don't you?"

"Yes. Poppa let me pick out the color myself."

Mason glanced back at Serena and Ben, who sat up straighter at the sound of the unfamiliar voice coming from Faith.

"What's your name?" Unable to contain his excitement, his question came out in a rush.

"Anna."

Mason let out a breath at the confidence of her answer. Drawing a blank on what he should ask next, he thought of the experience with the father. "Where is your Poppa now?"

"I don't know. Maybe the lumberyard, he comes and goes." She sounded indifferent.

"He works there?"

"He owns it."

Mason, not sure if that was significant, altered his questioning back to her. "Do you like gardenias?"

The blush on her cheeks was instant, and she gave a soft laugh. "Yes, he leaves them for me to find."

"Who does, Anna?"

"It's a secret. Poppa doesn't like me talking to him." Her voice now a whisper, Mason leaned closer to the bed.

"His name, Anna."

"No, Poppa might hear." Her agitation was evident with the tensing of her muscles. Her head turned slightly as if listening for the footsteps.

Turning himself to look towards the door, Mason waited for it to fly open again. Serena's huge eyes pleaded with him, as she shook her head.

"It's ok, Anna." Mason kept his voice even as he tried to reassure her. "Poppa is at work. At the lumberyard. Where is your mother?"

"Gone."

"Gone where?"

"She died." The sadness in her voice washed over him like a wave.

"Who else lives here with you?"

"The maid. Sometimes we have visitors, but

Poppa doesn't like it."

"Anna, how old are you?"

"16."

"The one who gives you flowers, is he here too?"

"No. Poppa doesn't want him in the house."

"Where do you meet him?"

"The barn out back mostly." A shy smile crossed her face. "Sometimes down by the river."

"Why can't you tell me his name?" Mason prodded gently.

"Poppa will kill him if he finds out." Clearly distressed, the crease on her forehead deepened.

"Does he work for your father at the lumber yard?" Mason knew he was grasping, but he needed to keep her talking about him.

"No, he helped build this house, and he takes care of the horses. I sneak out to the barn sometimes to see him. He likes my pies." The deep blush returned to her cheeks.

"Tell me his name." Mason tried to keep his voice level, but his impatience was winning out.

Her lidded eyes darted from side to side frantically. "No, I hear him. He's coming."

Mason watched Faith's chest rise and fall rapidly, her breath coming out in short spurts.

"Faith, Faith. I want you to wake up now." Mason's voice was sharp and commanding. He silently cursed himself for not adding a waking suggestion to his induction script.

"He's on the stairs." Her head cocked to one side as if listening. She panted shallowly, her hands clawed at the bed spread under her.

"Faith! Wake up!" Clapping his hands loudly, he repeated his command.

Faith gave a sharp intake of breath, and held her chest. "What?" her voice cracked as she tried to sit up slowly. "What happened? Did I fall asleep?"

"What do you remember?" Narrowing his eyes on her, Mason took note of the distinctive differences in their speech patterns.

"I must have been dreaming. Did it work? Did I remember anything?"

"Faith calm down. Everything is fine." Serena spoke from her seat in the corner of the room.

"What were you dreaming about?" Ben asked eagerly, making sure the recorder was still running.

"It's not real clear like it was before." Putting a palm out, Faith waved it slowly in front of her. "But it was the house. I was walking through the house looking for someone. There was a pie in the kitchen. I'm so confused."

"It's ok." Crossing the room to her, Serena patted her shoulder. Over Faith's head, she gave Ben a firm nod. "That's enough."

"I usually remember everything so clearly." Rubbing a hand across her eyes, Faith shook her head.

"Let's go downstairs and get you some water. Maybe it'll come back to you." Serena smiled reassuringly at her, and helped her from the bed.

Ben waited for them to leave the room before speaking. "Wow! That was the ghost talking, wasn't it? She's channeling the girl."

"Yes, I think so." Mason glanced around the room. The pale yellow walls glowed in the candlelight and the gardenia scent hung heavily in the air. Still, he felt a lingering sense of sadness.

"Can she do it again?"

"I don't know, Ben. Just keep recording everything."

Mason waited in the dimly lit parlor for Serena to come back inside. She had walked Faith to her car. He paced as he thought about the session. Faith was still a little shaky, but seemed more upset because she thought the session hadn't worked. He wasn't sure he should tell her that it had worked better than any of them could have imaged. He heard the door, but didn't bother to call out. Serena made a beeline for him.

"We're not doing that again." Her voice was firm, but low.

"Rena..," he sighed.

"No, Mason. That wasn't Faith and I don't like it. I can't use her that way." Crossing her arms in front of her, she shivered.

"Of course. I know you're upset but we have a name and a little more information."

"Upset? She's my friend."

"The voice wasn't hers. I know it's unnerving." He reached for her, sliding a hand across the goosebumps that had formed on her tanned skin.

"It was too easy. I don't like it."

"The night Jake and her brother fought, you said it wasn't her voice, correct?"

"Yes, I thought it was over. I thought all of them being here and all of the strong emotions just exploded. I thought it was what she needed to happen for it to be over." She leaned into him, and he welcomed the warmth of her on his chest.

"Ok, love. We'll figure it out." Wrapping his arms around her, he pulled her even closer. "Ben will go through the recordings and we'll see if we picked anything else up. Any news on the wedding?"

"Not really. I met with Claire today at her house. We talked about setting up outside and the food, but that's Faith's department. Why?"

"Serena, I know how much this means to you. I want this to work for you."

She stepped away from him to look into his eyes, "Really?"

"Yes. Your happiness is important to me."

"Why?" There was no accusation or suspicion in her question, just a genuine curiosity.

"Because we are going to work this out, one way or another."

"Are you so certain of that?" The uncertainty in her voice pained him.

"Yes. You know. From the moment we saw each other we both knew." Taking her chin in his hand, he stared deeply into her eyes.

She returned his gaze, her face softened. "Yes, we know the past, but the future is unwritten."

Not wanting to argue, he shook his head and looked away. "Then why do we keep finding each other, if it's not meant to be?"

"We keep repeating the past." She took a few steps, putting more space between them. "You think it's something we have to work on, but what if it's not?"

His hands still outstretched to her, he paused, confused at her meaning. "What are you talking about?"

"You keep telling me that I'm too close. That's

why I can't see what's going on here."

"Yes," he agreed slowly dropping his hands to his sides.

"What if you're too close to see what's happening with us?"

"I don't understand. What are you getting at?" His brow furrowed at the uncomfortable sensation going through him.

"What if we're repeating the cycle and that's what we need to work on?" Her voice was low, and cautious.

"Repeating the cycle?"

"Not repeating the cycle," she corrected him then waited for the realization to sink in.

"No." Moaning in protest, his insides felt like they were being ripped from him.

"We're trying to break the cycle for Anna and Faith, so they'll have peace. Maybe, we have to break the cycle with us, so we can finally have peace."

"No, Rena." His voice cracked as he pleaded with her.

"Don't we deserve some peace? Instead of torturing each other?" The sadness in her voice, made him want to howl. Life without her seemed impossible. His emotions roiled and simmered within him, he needed to get away before he lost control. He stopped only for a second as he passed her, shoulder to shoulder. Not able to look at her, he looked straight ahead.

"There is no peace for me, without you."

CHAPTER 11

Serena wondered if the others were awake as she made her way to the kitchen. The only sounds she heard were Faith's usual clattering. Upon entering, she took in Ben at his usual spot already eating. There was no sign of Mason.

"Is Mason not joining us for breakfast?" Serena tried to hide her disappointment by giving Ben a cheery smile.

"Oh. Umm, no." Ben looked guilty down at his plate.

"What?" She knew she had hurt Mason last night. She had almost followed him out of the house, but she knew how it would end. More angry words and hurt feelings.

"I thought he talked to you before he left." Ben shifted uncomfortably in his seat, he glanced nervously at Faith's back. Breakfast already made, she was on to her next task.

"He left?" Her journey to the coffee pot derailed by his statement, Serena stood still. It wasn't like Mason to run away or give up.

"Yeah, he said y'all had agreed to hold off on the sessions with Faith," Ben spoke calmly watching her face.

"Why? It didn't work, right? I knew it." Finding the bowl she needed, Faith snapped the cabinet door shut, her head bobbing in frustration.

"No, Faith, because it worked too well," Ben informed her.

"I don't understand. I don't remember anything. Just pie." She snorted, flipping her ponytail with another jerk of her head.

"Just show her." Ben's blue eyes urged her, his boyish face barely able to contain his excitement.

"I don't think that's necessary." Serena gave Ben a forced smile then tried to change the subject. "What else did Mason say?"

"Something about stepping back and giving you space. He said for me to stay here, work on EVPs, since we never got around to it and I still want to check out the graveyard." Napkin in hand he shrugged, wiping his mouth.

"When will he be back?"

"Ahhh, he didn't say, but he will. You know he will." He rolled the napkin nervously between his hands.

"Good. We've got a lot of planning to do for the

wedding. Have you gotten with Claire yet? She had some ideas about the food." Trying to focus on their to-do list, she addressed Faith. If Mason wasn't around, she might actually be able to focus on what needed to be done. This wedding had to happen.

"We talked, and you're right. We have a lot to do."

"Evan and Claire ok?"

"Yeah. Evan's sulking, but Claire stood her ground. She's determined to keep planning. She told him there's been no sign of Richie. Right?" Faith looked at them over the ingredients she had gathered.

"Nothing, really." Serena cast a warning glance to Ben. "Richie isn't going to be a problem. Let's just focus on the wedding."

"Ok, we should go dress shopping. That'll cheer Claire up!"

The dream came back to her in a rush. The three of them laughing amidst a sea of white satin, taffeta, and tulle. Their dresses each as unique as their personalities. Claire's satin dress draped around her curves giving her the look of a '50s bombshell. Faith's more traditional lace gown boasted a sweetheart neckline, capped sleeves and a fluted skirt ending in an elegant train. She had found herself in lace also, but a simpler style. No train, but the fitted bodice had ended at her hips giving way to a full skirt. The off-the-shoulder ruffle blowing into her face with a cold gust of wind.

Suddenly darkness surrounded them. Their stark white dresses almost glowing in contrast to the blackness. The laughter had dried up and a feeling of dread engulfed her. Claire cried out startling her. A splatter of blood had appeared on the bodice of her beautiful satin gown. The darkness forced them apart, leaving her all alone. Claire's cries echoed throughout the house. She searched frantically through each room trying to find her friend, only to awaken in a panic.

"Serena, hey?"

"Hmm." She found herself standing in the brightly lit kitchen amid the smells of breakfast and coffee.

"Where did you go?" Ben eyed her worriedly.

"Oh, I just remembered something. The dresses. Yes, Claire needs a dress." Her mind still not fully present, she replied absently.

"We all will." Faith snorted over a cup of flour.

Their white dresses flashed again before her. Panic began to rise and she felt the darkness creeping around her.

"For the wedding. Bridesmaids." Faith raised an eyebrow at her. "What's up with you?"

"I remembered the dream."

"Oh… Wow." Wiping a hand on her apron, Faith stared at her in awe.

"What dream?" Ben asked pushing his plate away.

"It's nothing."

"Did you write it down? I don't remember anything about a dream."

"No, it was before. It wasn't about that." Serena shook her head. How could she have forgotten about the dream?

"It was Richie," Faith offered.

The incredulous look Ben gave her made her rethink what she just said. "Oh, Ben. I thought it was over. It happened."

"What happened?"

Serena relayed the dream in as much detail as she could remember.

"Wow, so this was before Richie showed up?"

"Yes, I had read Claire's cards. They warned her about Richie."

"So, now, we're talking about dresses again. White dresses. Planning a wedding and I'm assuming you and Jake have plans to get married too?" Ben asked Faith.

"Yeah, but not until Claire and Evan are safely wed." She sliced the stick of butter in one motion, then pulled at the paper unrolling it into the bowl with a plop.

"Following the natural progression of the dream's meaning..." He patiently rolled his hand in a circle. The innocent look he gave Serena made her want to throw something at him.

"No, Ben. We were trying on dresses." Reaching for a cup, she hoped the coffee would clear her head.

"You said that was the order y'all would get married in. Claire, Faith, then you," he repeated her own words to make his point.

"Ugh, but it happened already. Richie came and threatened to mess everything up. Claire was missing for a while, but we found her. Evan found her. So it's over." Serena poured the dark liquid into her cup wishing her words were true.

"And now he's back. There's two weddings being planned and y'all are trying on dresses."

"It doesn't mean something will happen." She didn't look at him when she answered. Staring into the blackness in her cup, the surface now smooth and still, just like the air around her. But it was a false sense of calmness. Serena knew it was only a matter of time before something else bubbled to the surface.

"Hey, maybe not. I'm just pointing out stuff, like I always do when y'all can't see it." He shrugged his shoulders and looked down at his empty plate. "You know, I really don't blame Evan for not wanting Claire here or the wedding."

Ben picked up his plate, bringing it to the sink with a frown. "I'm going upstairs to grab some equipment, then I'm heading to the graveyard."

After he left the room, Serena waited for Faith to say something, anything to erase the doubts that were creeping in. When Faith stayed silent, Serena spoke, "Don't listen to him. I know it's going to be fine."

"I just want this to work." Faith flipped the dough out of the bowl and unto the counter pounding it with her fist.

"I do, too." Amazed at the dough that had magically seemed to appear, Serena watched her friend knead it quickly.

"Is Claire safe?" Her attention fully on Serena now, Faith asked with genuine concern.

"Yes, he can't hurt her anymore."

"How do you know?"

"Because it's me he's after."

"But we all saw him." Rounding the dough back into a ball, Faith patted it gently.

"I was so nervous about that party. He used my fear."

"Hey." Ben strode back into the kitchen startling them both. "I forgot, with Mason leaving, I edited the pictures for Claire and..." He hesitated looking at the top picture. Finally pulling it from the stack he handed it to Serena. "Look at this. I took this when

Claire was at the top of the stairs."

"I'm sure that's not what she wanted to remember, Reuben." She snatched the photo from his hand.

Faith leaned over her shoulder to get a better look and gasped. The shadowy form of a man stood behind a terrified Claire on the staircase. "It came out."

"Yeah, it did. And I didn't mean for Claire to have that. I wanted you to see it." Ben put the stack of pictures on the counter.

"See what?" Serena snapped at him.

"See what you and Mason tend to forget. What normal people see. For you it's no big deal. For Claire and Evan, especially Evan, it's pretty damn scary." His voice was calm, but firm.

Looking at the photo again, the shadow, a thing of darkness so close to Claire it could have touched her. Serena felt the darkness circling her again.

"Point taken."

CHAPTER 12

Mason powered the sleek Lincoln MKZ through a final gentle s-curve on Highway 35. The close looming cypress and water oaks thinned quickly as the road straightened out before him. Miles of flat, neatly rowed cane and bean fields stretched out ahead. He nudged the cruise control to a dicey seventy-five and let his mind relax into autopilot.

Leaving her and that damn house was hard, but Mason knew where to find her now. Ben was right. He needed to get his head on straight, and Serena wouldn't leave Coeur du Bayou.

Storming out of the house last night, he had paced through the woods sulking. The darkness and summer night sounds did little to calm him. The constant buzzing and bites from hungry mosquitos had driven him back to his room. He needed to figure out a way to prove to her they were meant to be together. Serena was wrong. She had to be. Somewhere in the wee hours of the morning he had come to the conclusion that he should start with the trust issue. The missing money and the deliberate set up of that investigation bothered him. If he could clear her, he would have no reason not to trust her.

There had been a plan, but somewhere in the haze of no sleep and the panic of a life without her, he lost it. Mason felt he needed to go home and sort it out. He was only an hour away, when his cell phone buzzed in the console, irritating him more. Ben's name glowed on the screen. He took a deep breath then clicked the hands-free button.

"Hey, what's up?"

"Mason, hey, listen… Maybe you should come back." He could tell Ben was trying to be casual.

"What's happened?" Slowing the car, Mason began looking for the next exit. Ben wouldn't ask him to come back unless it was serious.

"Nothing yet, but Serena just told me some disturbing stuff. Do you trust her dreams?"

"Dreams?" Relieved, he coasted down the exit looking for a place to park.

Pulling into a restaurant parking lot, he listened to Ben describe Serena's dream. The thought of Serena in a white dress made him feel weird. The blood on the dress and Richie returning made his blood boil.

"So, she's saying the night Richie died, Claire went missing and they found the graveyard, was her dream?"

"Yes."

"But you think it's not over. Why?" Trying to understand Ben's concern, his gaze wandered to the flashing arrow sign.

"They're planning to go dress shopping. Wedding dress shopping."

"What?" The image of Serena in a flowing white dress came to mind again. "Do you really think something will happen? I don't know, Ben."

"Look, I'm going out to the graveyard. We might be missing something there."

"Why do I need to come back? If they're going shopping, they won't be at the house."

"Serena is planning to have dresses brought to Coeur du Bayou for them to try on."

"Why? Is she trying to provoke him?"

"I don't know, but she's not telling us everything. I had to practically drag the dream out of her."

"I'm coming back. Let me call Sebastian. We might need help." Mason already reaching for the key in the ignition, made the decision instantly. He wasn't sure what Serena had in mind, but he'd rather be close by.

"Yeah, if you think so."

"What?" Ben's less than enthusiastic response had him questioning his decision.

"Just maybe, Gabe might be more helpful. If you think we need help."

Mason sighed as he made the connection Ben was trying to point out. Sebastian was an unapologetic ladies man. He flirted shamelessly with every female he came in contact with. After meeting Evan, it was sure to be trouble down the road.

"Yeah, you're right. Sorry, I wasn't thinking."

"Look, just come back. You might get something

that's not obvious to Serena. Or maybe figure out what she's up to."

"Up to?" The suspicion rose up quickly, and he cursed himself for it.

"I can't understand it. She doesn't want her friends hurt, but she's going ahead with this. Maybe she just doesn't see it."

Ben was trying to reason it out for himself. Mason could hear the sharp click of his camera. Obviously at the graveyard, he was determined to keep moving forward.

"Oh, Rena..," Mason whispered half to himself. "She does Ben. She knows exactly what she's doing."

"I don't."

"She's showing him she's not afraid." He remembered the fierceness in her eyes when she cursed Richie for coming into her home. No, she wouldn't let him take over, but foolishly her friends would be there, too. "Ok, I'll come back. Maybe we can distract her with Anna."

"She doesn't want to do that again," Ben reminded him.

"Well, then maybe we'll try with Jake."

Mason had plenty of time on the drive back to Coeur du Bayou to go over everything leading up to the time Serena had run off.

When he brought her home with him, everything had been fine. There had been some awkwardness, sure. Ending his engagement to Eva so abruptly had been a shock to his family, but they had all warmed to Serena immediately. Sebastian a little too much.

Mason's feelings for her had been so overwhelming he had fought with Sebastian. His jealousy quickly drove a wedge between them. Sebastian's need for attention had him flirting with Serena just to spite him.

The team was promising. With the rise of reality TV in the ratings and so much talent on their team, he knew their chances of getting their own show were better than good. Eva, his ex-fiancé had been the one pushing them into the TV show. Actually, he had suspected it was Sebastian's idea from the beginning. His little brother had used Eva to get him to agree to the idea. Sebastian had always longed for the limelight, and Eva was ambitious. Her business sense and confidence had appealed to him when they first met.

By the time Eva was out of the picture, they were well on the road to TV-land. With stars in their eyes, they set up an investigation at a notoriously haunted house. They began their work like any other job, but this time with cameras in their faces. It was challenging, especially for Ben, who really preferred to be behind the camera, but they all soon adjusted to their roles as would-be celebrity ghost hunters.

Then, just as they became comfortable with constant surveillance and camera crews under foot, funding was pulled, and a lawsuit threatened. Then Serena disappeared and he discovered the money was also gone.

His first instinct was to blame Sentinel, a rival ghost hunting team, but when the money disappeared, too, he had to rethink. Serena leaving so suddenly, right at that crucial time, had him drawing obvious conclusions.

Pulling his bags out of the car, his eyes were drawn to the house. Serena's house. Something wasn't sitting well with him. The jealousy maybe. The front door opened, and the frantic look on Ben's face alarmed him.

"Mason… Man." Running a hand through his closely cropped hair, Ben sighed with relief.

"What is it?"

"She had another episode in the kitchen."

Hurrying to the kitchen, he found Faith sitting on the floor, her back propped against a cabinet. Evidence of tears showed on her face.

"What happened?"

"It was so real…," she whispered.

"Tell me."

"The recorder's running," Ben said in a soft voice behind him. "The meters went off down here. I thought it was an earthquake or something."

"Tell me," Mason prompted Faith again as he sat next to her on the floor.

"Pie. I was making a pie for him. I sneaked it out to the barn for him. I was going to leave it there. He leaves gardenias there for me."

"Ok. The barn is close by then. Here on the property?"

"I think so, yes." Faith sniffed rubbing at her nose.

"You left the pie?"

"He was waiting for me." She smiled sadly. "We… We're in love, but my father can't find out. He doesn't like him because he's from across the river. After, we…" Her cheeks bloomed with color and she looked down shyly. "I walked him to the ferry. Through the woods so no one would see us together."

"Ferry?" Mason didn't like the way she kept

slipping from her own thoughts into this new persona.

"He lives across the river and only comes to town to work."

"Why were you crying? Were you scared?" Mason reached for her hand, holding it gently in his. He sensed a subtle variation in her speech pattern as she shifted from her own agitated reaction to the eerily calm thoughts, feelings and memories of Anna.

"No, I'm sad," Faith continued, now firmly in Anna's aspect.

"The baby?" he asked, suddenly feeling a sorrow that was deep and overwhelming. It hung on his shoulders like a weight pulling him to the ground.

"No, my mother died upstairs." Faith pointed to the ceiling. "She's been so sick since we moved here."

"She showed you her mother dying." He squeezed her hand, knowing the pain she had just experienced.

Faith stalled in her reply. A surge of painful regret rippled across her face. In a beat she refocused and met his gaze. "She was with him when her mother died. She's so sad and she wanted to go back to him, but she has to wait until he comes for her."

"Where is everybody?" Serena's voice echoed through the foyer.

"In here," Ben called out.

"Hey, I thought you were..." Her dark eyes took in Mason, and Faith on the floor. "I told you to leave her alone."

"We didn't do this. She was in here alone when it happened." Ben used his patient voice as he clicked off the recorder.

"Anna wants her to see," Mason said simply watching her face change from anger to understanding.

"Anna?" Faith asked softly.

"The ghost lady." Serena smiled sadly as she knelt down to be eye level with Faith.

"Oh. Her name. How did you find it? On the grave?" Looking to Ben, Faith gulped loudly.

"Umm..." Ben looked uncomfortably from Mason to Serena. "No, you told us."

"No, I didn't know her name. Did I say that?" Rubbing her head, she sat up straighter trying to recall.

"Not today, hun. In the session," Serena answered, her dark curls hid her face as she hung her head. She knew what was coming next, and Mason could tell she wasn't happy about it.

"I want to see the video."

CHAPTER 13

"This isn't a good idea." Serena cast a worried glance at Mason over Faith's head, who sat next to her on the love seat fidgeting.

"I agree, but she wants to see it." Mason paced the parlor floor waiting for Ben to return with his laptop.

"Yes, I do. I don't remember anything really. This time it was so clear. I was there." Faith wrung her hands.

"Rena, obviously the ghost is going to show us one way or another." Mason could feel Serena's dread. Once Faith saw the video everything could fall apart. If what she saw frightened her, she might leave

Coeur du Bayou never to return.

"I want Jake here. He should be here," Faith announced rubbing her hands on her jeans.

"We talked about this." Serena was quick to caution her friend.

"Please, do a session with him. I need to know." Grabbing Serena's hands in hers, Faith pleaded desperately.

"Know what?" Obviously surprised by Faith's surge of emotion, Serena's brow furrowed with concern.

"It's him, isn't it? I'm her and he's the guy." With watery eyes, Faith looked from Serena to Mason for confirmation.

"No, Faith. Just calm down." Serena shook her head making her curls fall forward over her shoulders.

"I can't. I felt it. It was real!" Pulling her hands away from Serena, Faith rubbed them over her face.

"Ok. I'll just set this on the table." Ben held out his laptop as he entered the room, stopping at the awkward silence.

"I called Jake," Faith blurted out.

"What? When?"

"I want him to see. Maybe he'll remember."

"I could just bring the laptop to him," Ben offered lamely.

"No, he's on his way." Faith's determination was clear. Mason watched her closely. If she was acting strangely, surely Serena would notice. As soon as the front door opened Faith jumped up off the sofa, meeting Jake as he entered the room.

"Hey, babe. What's going on?" His brown eyes were focused only on Faith.

"I'm ok. I had another episode."

"Oh. So you're ok?" Still in his work clothes, Jake regarded them nervously before pulling Faith towards him.

"Yeah, I'm ok, now." Faith wrapped her arms around his waist.

"You need me to take you home?" Jake asked softly into her hair.

"No, I want you to watch this with me." At Faith's request, Jake looked over her head questioningly.

"It's a video of her session. I'm still not sure she should see it." Serena stood making her objection clear.

"Why? What happened?"

"Umm, nothing. She just answered some questions," Ben answered, setting up his laptop on an end table.

"But I don't even remember the questions or answering them. That's why I want to see it." Faith's voice was persuasive, her ponytail swayed with each shake of her head.

"How come she doesn't remember?" Jake asked nervously.

"It's common with hypnosis." Mason could feel Jake's uneasiness. With the past experiences his apprehension was understandable.

"Oh yeah, I think I had heard that somewhere." Pulling at his work shirt, he noticed his clothes. "I should have stopped to take a shower first. I just.... You sounded upset on the phone."

"I'm ok, really." Faith gave him a quick peck on the cheek then turned to Ben. "Can we do this?"

"Faith..," Serena started to object again.

"Rena, she wants to see it and there's really no

reason for her not to. Maybe it'll put their minds at ease." Mason reached out a hand to touch her shoulder, he longed for more. He wanted to comfort her, to hold her.

Glancing over her shoulder at him, she nodded. "Go ahead then. I'll be in the kitchen."

Letting out a sigh, he followed her a few steps to the foyer. It seemed one of them was always walking away.

Suddenly turning to face him fully, Serena grabbed his arm. The heat was instantaneous. "I thought you left?"

"I thought I needed to leave. Right now, I think me being here for you is more important." Mason stared into her eyes. Their connection went beyond words.

She let go of his arm and nodded silently before leaving the room. Mason wanted to follow her out, to tell her she was wrong about them. Instead he focused on the room around him. Traces of lingering sadness, and something else he couldn't place.

Ben sat Jake and Faith down on the love seat and pulled an end table with the laptop in front of them. Once they were settled, Ben started the video. Mason knew Ben was watching them closely for signs of distress. He heard his own voice telling Faith to relax and he felt the room again. Something felt off to him.

When Anna started answering him, he heard Jake's sharp intake of breath. Jake took hold of Faith's hand as the questioning continued. Finally, the video ended. Everyone sat in silence waiting for Faith to say something.

"Her name is Anna." Faith smiled at Jake squeezing his hand. Excitement was not what Mason had expected.

"Yeah, that was weird." Jake pulled at his shirt with his free hand, and looked down at this shoes.

"Jake, you ok?" Ben asked concerned.

"Yeah, it was just weird seeing her like that."

"Yes, it can be unsettling," Mason tried to reassure him.

"Can we go now?" Jake asked Faith directly.

"Yeah, sure. Let me get my stuff and tell Serena bye." Faith left the room, a happy smile on her face.

Jake immediately stood and faced him. "What was that? It wasn't her voice!"

"Calm down, Jake. She was under hypnosis." Ben closed the laptop and stood.

"I don't like it. Don't do it again." Unconsciously he pulled at his shirt repeatedly.

"Serena has voiced the same concerns, so we've decided not to proceed with the sessions. So we're good." Mason gave him a friendly smile.

"Serena didn't want her to?" Dropping his hands to his hips, Jake's brow raised with suspicion.

"I told you. Her main concern is her friends." Trying his best to smooth over Jake's uneasiness, Mason shrugged calmly.

"Can't you just do an exorcism or something to get this over with?" Jake's voice was wrought with fear and desperation.

Mason felt the change in the air before he could answer. A door upstairs slammed. The light fixture overhead started to hum.

Faith and Serena came back into the parlor looking behind them nervously.

"You should go," Serena said to Jake.

"Yeah, good idea." Jake reached for Faith's arm,

still warily eyeing the light fixture. "Come on, babe."

"I think you should take a break for a few days, or so," Serena suggested, her eyes wandering from the ceiling back to Faith. "We all do. So take few days off from here. Don't worry about food, we'll be fine."

Ben grumbled, but nodded in agreement.

"Wait." Faith dug her feet into the antique rug when Jake tried to pull her to the door. "I'm not running away from this."

"Actually, I was thinking we'd all go away for a while. Mason has things to take care of and Ben has a lot of reviewing to do. Y'all should all go."

"Serena... No! We've got a wedding to plan, remember?" Faith ignored the slamming door. Overhead the hum grew louder.

"You and Claire can work on the food plans and whatever else." Serena tried again to corral them to the door.

"What about dresses?" Faith still wasn't budging.

"We can do that when I get back. There's plenty of time."

"Back?" Mason's curiosity mixed with a tinge of panic that she would leave this place and he wouldn't be able to find her again.

"I also have some business to take care of."

"Ok. I'll stay here and review and keep an eye on things for you," Ben offered.

"I don't need you to stay Ben." Serena obviously frustrated with Ben for voicing his intentions in front of Faith, crossed her arms in front of her.

"I know, but everything's here and set up already. I think I should just stay here."

"And y'all should take a trip to the city to go dress shopping. You'd have more to choose from,"

Mason suggested casually. His gaze was drawn to the candlestick on the mantle.

"You called him." Her eyes narrowed on Ben. "I knew it."

"I don't think it's a good idea, and I'm sure I'm not the only one," Ben defended his actions.

"Rena, we can talk about that later. After we all take a few days and come back. It'll give us all time to consider the evidence and figure out how to proceed." He envisioned taking Serena home with him, or just a few days on a beach somewhere. Images of their tanned bodies intertwined in the sand sprang to mind.

"I'm set up here. I'm not leaving." Ben shoved his hands in his pockets, and shrugged.

"Well, what about my baking?" Faith asked.

"You have a cake due soon?"

"No, but... What about.. Ugh." Faith slapped a hand to her forehead. "I was supposed to make pies for the diner."

"Faith, you can use my kitchen. Just for a few days. Gil will understand if you don't have any for tomorrow." Jake rubbed a hand over her arm.

"He might, but I don't." She yanked her arm away from Jake and glared at Serena. "What's different? It happened before. I'm fine."

"Look, let's just take a few days and come back."

"Ugh, whatever." With a final snort, Faith pushed Jake towards the heavy wooden door.

Once they were gone, Ben cleared his throat. "Um, ok. I'll let you guys talk."

"We don't need to," Serena snapped.

"Yes, we do. Where are you going?" Not able to help himself, the words were out like the panic clawing at him.

"That's none of your business. But you should take few days to see about your business." She gave him a sarcastic smile as she emphasized the last words.

Tightening his jaw, Mason nodded curtly. Not willing to argue again, he bit back his reply. She was his business. Everything about her from the soap she used to her favorite food would be his business.

"If it's alright with you, I need some sleep. I'll leave in the morning."

"Fine. Sweet dreams." Serena turned for the hidden doorway to her room. "I've got to pack."

"I hate it when Mommy and Daddy fight," Ben said in a small high pitched voice, hugging his laptop to him.

Mason laughed at the expression on Ben's face and he thought he caught a smirk on Serena's before the bookcase door snapped shut.

CHAPTER 14

The house was quiet. A little too quiet for Ben. The only thing worse than the quiet was the bickering. He hadn't been joking. He hated it when they fought. Mason and his family were the closest thing to a family Ben had left. Growing up, his family home had been filled with plenty of arguing and turmoil. Ben had learned to read people because of the constant drama and violence in his own family. Quickly realizing the importance of remaining calm and injecting levity in certain situations, he survived his teenage years unscathed. His family however, had not. Through the years, they had all left one by one, either by choice or death.

Meeting Mason had been a game changer for him. Mason had picked up on his ability and shown him the value of it. Mason, his brothers, and even his parents had accepted him without question. When Mason had brought Serena home, he could see their attraction went beyond the physical. Their team worked well together. Everyone left the technical stuff to him and that made him happy.

He was really happy that he didn't have to roll up all of the equipment. Ben settled in to review the tapes and recordings. His first day had been spent pouring over pictures looking for anomalies. Orbs were common. Several of the pictures of Faith and Jake together contained at least one orb.

Ben was in the process of renaming files when he heard a noise downstairs. He waited a heartbeat, listening and watching. The meters didn't move. He heard definite movement downstairs. Groaning, he went to investigate. Looking down from the landing, he wasn't surprised to see a wide eyed Claire glancing around nervously in the darkened foyer.

"What are you doing here?" His voice echoed off the high ceiling.

"Oh!" Claire jumped guiltily, clamping a hand over her mouth. Her big blue eyes found Ben descending the stairs to her. "Hey, I just came to… Umm… Pay you for the pictures. They came out so good. Is Serena here?"

"No. She had to go out of town and I don't need you to pay me. She did that already." He motioned her towards the door.

"Oh." She gulped nervously.

The distinctive clank of metal coming from the direction of the kitchen made Claire jump again.

"Are you kidding?" Ben groaned again making a beeline for the kitchen.

Apron clad and well into the mixing, a guilty Faith rubbed flour from her face.

"Are y'all trying to get me in trouble with Serena?"

"No, I was trying to be quiet. I have pies to make. I couldn't wait anymore." Noticing Claire behind him, she frowned. "Oh Claire. What are you doing here? Evan's gonna have a fit."

"I didn't see your car here, Faith." Claire put her purse on the edge of the counter ignoring both of their questions.

"I parked in the back."

"Ok.... You bake. I'll stay right here until you're through." Ben sat at the island eyeing Claire. "You. What are you really doing here?"

"I told you."

"Claire." He frowned at her.

"Ok. I thought maybe if I came and talked to Richie, he'd go away." Her blue eyes held sorrow, but also hope as she pleaded her case.

"Because that worked so well while he was alive." Faith snorted, turning back to her work.

"It might work, right?" Claire asked Ben, ignoring Faith's comment.

"I don't know. I just know you guys aren't supposed to be here and if something happens Serena will have my head."

"Why did you get to stay?" Faith narrowed her eyes at him over the pie pan.

"I have a lot of video and audio to go over. Packing up didn't make any sense. I'd just have to come back and set it all back up. It wasn't practical."

"Can we at least try it?" Claire smiled at him.

"Try what?"

"Talking to Richie."

"No, not without Serena and Mason here. One of them should be here." Regretting his decision to stay, he shook his head firmly.

"Why do you need them?"

"I'm not like them. I can't feel spirits like they do." Noticing Claire's pout, he added, "I am sensitive to some things, but they're more in tune. And again, Serena will have my head."

"I still can't believe she never told us." Claire pouted leaning against the counter. "So what can we do?"

"Plan your wedding." Splaying his hands out in front of him on the counter, he leaned forward emphasizing each word.

"If we don't get rid of Richie, Evan will never allow the wedding here." Faith turned to place the empty mixing bowl into the sink.

"Is that a big deal? Maybe you should think about having it somewhere else." His eyes were on Claire. He never saw the rag coming. It hit him square in the mouth, splattering soapy water across his face and down his shirt. Blinking away the droplets from his eyes, he asked, "What was that for?"

"It is a big deal! It's her wedding and our business. Don't be a jerk!"

"Woah, ok. Let's calm down, Betty Crocker." Ben put his hands up in surrender.

Claire giggled, breaking the tension. Faith rolled her eyes then smirked at him. "Ok, but you've got to help us. We want to help, too."

"God, help me." Seeing the determination on

their faces, he knew there was no talking them out of it.

―――――――

"This is a bad idea," Ben voiced his concern out loud, but the girls weren't paying attention to him. Faith was busy cleaning up while they waited for the last few minutes on the timer to go by. Keeping an eye out for flying objects, he muttered to himself all of the reasons he should make them leave.

While Faith had worked on the pies, he had gotten Claire's account of what had happened on Halloween night when Richie showed up. Serena hadn't recorded anything about Richie. Obviously wanting them all to forget the horrible ordeal.

Claire had been reluctant to talk about Richie, but with a little prodding she had finally opened up. He needed to know the details if they were actually going to go through with it. The look on Faith's face made it clear to him that Claire hadn't told any of them how bad her relationship with Richie had been. Richie was some piece of work. No wonder Evan didn't want her here.

"This is a bad idea," he repeated thinking of the temper that apparently ran in their family. Evan would not be throwing dish rags. "Really bad idea."

Claire jumped when the timer dinged. Faith hurried over to the oven, mitts in hand. Expertly retrieving the pie and placing them on cooling racks, she addressed Ben through the steam. "Look, it's worth a try, right? It can't hurt."

"I don't know. From what Rena has told me, he thinks she pushed him down the stairs to steal the money."

"Why her? Why not me?" Claire asked confused.

"It's my understanding that you left the house to draw him outside."

"Yeah, I did. But she didn't do it. Evan got here and found him."

"That's what she said, but for some reason he's fixated on her." Shrugging his shoulders, he was glad for the conversation. Maybe he could drag it out to delay their plan.

"So, we should do this now?" A wide eyed Claire dashed his hopes.

"Umm, yeah, if y'all want." Ben had been watching her. She was nervous and spooked, not a good combination.

"Yes we do, Ben. Let's get to it," Faith answered firmly pulling the apron over her head.

Sighing he gave in. "Ok, this is how it's going to work." He held up an EMF meter and handed it to Faith. "You hold this, and watch the numbers."

"I can do that."

"What do I do?"

"You will ask questions."

"Questions?"

"Yes, you need to talk to Richie, but put it in question form so he will answer you. That's the idea anyway. After each question, you need to be silent for a few seconds to give him a chance to answer."

Claire gulped loudly. "Will I hear him?"

"No, probably not. We won't know if it worked until I run it through a processor. Once we decide the best place to do this, I'll set the video camera up, too." Giving them both time to change their minds, he waited a few beats. "I'm thinking the staircase."

Claire gulped again.

"We don't have to do this, Claire."

"No, I want to," Claire answered firmly, then bit her lip. "Do I have to go up the stairs?"

"No, it's safer if you just stand on the bottom step."

"Ok, yeah. That's good."

"So let's go set it up." Faith pushed Claire towards the door.

Ben followed them into the foyer wondering how he had gotten himself into this mess. He took his time setting up the video camera on the tripod thinking he'd give them another chance to back out.

"It's also important for everyone to stay calm. If you get really scared or angry," he gave Faith a sidelong glance before continuing, "they can feed off of those emotions. So stay calm."

"Ok." Claire pursed her lips in determination. She stepped on to the step and stood with her back straight.

"This is Ben Peltier, here with Faith..." Sending Faith a questioning look over the camera, he motioned for her to supply her name.

"Faith Williams."

Ben pointed at Claire.

"Claire Hebert." Claire's voice broke a little as she squeaked out her name.

"Claire will be asking questions. Claire, whenever you're ready."

"Oh." Claire gulped again looking around nervously. "Richie, are you here?"

After a few seconds she gave Ben a questioning look. He nodded for her to continue. She cleared her throat and took a deep breath.

"Richie, it's Claire. We don't have your money. The police took it."

Ben frowned at her. "Questions, remember?"

"Oh, yeah," she said softly. "Richie, why are you here?"

Faith pointed to the meter. Ben could tell from the lights something was happening.

"Richie, what do you want?"

After almost a minute, Claire frowned at Ben. "I guess I should have wrote some questions down."

"Maybe you should ask him what hell feels like," Faith snorted.

Ben rolled his eyes at Faith over the camera.

Claire took a seat on the bottom step. "I know you came here because of the money, right?"

Biting her lip, she continued. "Did you ever love me?"

Taken back by her question, Ben looked away. The question was a little more personal than he was used to on an investigation.

"Claire," he whispered.

"I just wondered. I think I know the answer, but I just can't help but think there was some good in there somewhere. Even if just at the beginning." Sighing, she straightened her shoulders again.

"Richie, do you know I'm getting married? I'm so happy. For once, I'm actually happy and you are not going to ruin this for me. You need to go!"

"Ok, Claire. That's good." Uncomfortable with the tears in her eyes, he figured it was time to shut it down. "Faith give me the meter. You two should go. I'll pick this up."

"Oh," Claire's disappointment was clear. "Do you think we got something?"

"I won't know until I go back over it." He held his hand out for the meter. Faith frowned but handed it over. "Besides the EMF meter going off, there's no evidence of anything, but..."

A door slammed upstairs.

"Oh, man. Y'all need to go." Holding out a hand to Claire, he pulled her to her feet. The meter in his other hand started going nuts.

"Faith!" Claire exclaimed, pushing him out of the way. Faith lay crumpled on the floor, exactly how he had found her a few days before in the kitchen.

CHAPTER 15

Not bothering to stop at his apartment, Mason headed straight to the family home. The expansive Spanish Revival estate his grandfather built in the '20s boasted of his family's lineage straight back to one of the original families sent by the king of Spain, himself, to settle the area. His parents' estate would always be home to him and his brothers. No matter how far they traveled, they knew they had a place here. Mason waited in the great room, he knew his mother would be expecting him.

"Where the hell have you been?" Gabriel, Mason's older brother, was never one to mince words. Entering the great room, he headed for the bar. Taller by a few inches, his brother favored their father with his lanky build, whereas, Mason took after his mother's side of the family. Even though Gabe was only a few years older, he sported more than a few gray hairs. Mason assumed it had to do with the stress of taking over several of the hotel properties after their father had fallen ill a few years ago. Laurent Del Toro, a classic workaholic, had not only expanded their family's fortune over the years but also accumulated enough arterial plaque to cause a stroke. At their mother's urging, he had reluctantly handed over a substantial portion of his responsibilities to his sons.

"Personal business." From his comfy position on the vintage loveseat, Mason waited for the ribbing to commence.

"Personal?" His scrutinizing gaze often made Mason wonder if Gabe didn't have a touch of intuitiveness also. "You found her then?"

"Yes. We're trying to work things out." The sly look Gabe gave him made Mason pause. "What?"

"Yet, you are here…," looking around the room, then behind the bar for emphasis before continuing, "and she's not."

"Don't be an ass."

His brother's good hearted chuckle grated on his nerves. Mason knew Gabe didn't really understand his tie to Serena. None of them did. How could they?

"Well, since you're here, let me run this by you. I'm thinking of setting up an investigation." Ice clinked in his tumbler as he poured a finger of the amber colored liquid.

"Really?" Taken aback by his brother's announcement, his curiosity was aroused. Gabe, being the skeptic, usually didn't seek out haunted places. "Where?"

"Nearby. I doubt we get anything. Their claims are more for the tourists I imagine."

"Do you need me then?" His thoughts flew to Serena and Coeur du Bayou. He didn't want anything to get in the way of their reconciliation.

"I would say no, but it would be great having you and Serena there to debunk this for me."

"Talk about personal." He considered his brother motives. Judging by his tense shoulders and lined forehead, it was a thorn in his side. "Ah, it is. Rival?"

"They shouldn't have thrown out a challenge if they can't back it up." Gabe paced in front of the mantel of their parents' greatroom. This was home base, for all of them.

"Challenge?"

"Yes. Stay the night, you know the drill."

"Mmmm, yes." Mason smiled at his brother. An easy challenge for their team. Gabe didn't believe. Mason could sense and Ben wanted proof desperately. They had no problem staying overnight. As tempting as it sounded, he couldn't stay away from Serena for long. He needed to get back to her and Coeur du Bayou. The anger in that house chilled him. He opened his mouth to tell Gabe about Serena's house and what he had experienced in such a short time, but stopped.

"What?" Gabe eyed him expectantly.

"Hmm?"

"You were about to say something. It looked important." Taking a seat in the armchair across from Mason, Gabe gave him his full attention.

"Oh, nothing. Have you told Sebastian yet?"

"When I see him." Gabe sat back in the arm chair with a sigh. "It won't be until the fall. You know, the Halloween hype."

"Where is he?" Knowing Sebastian, it was somewhere with lots of pretty women and an overflowing bar.

"Funny, you didn't ask about Ben. I thought you three had run off on some wild getaway." Frowning, Gabe took a swig of his drink.

Mason laughed at his brother's word choice. "And why would you not be invited?"

"Yeah, right."

"Seriously, Gabriel. You are quite the level headed businessman, but I bet when you cut loose, it's got to be a spectacle." Mason thought of the younger version of his brother. There had been a time when he was more wild and carefree.

"Someone has got to keep things going around here."

"Where's Dad?"

"He should be on a cruise enjoying his twilight years with his beautiful wife." His mother's voice floated before her into the great room, accompanied by the sound of her heels clicking on the tile floor. Mason stood instantly to greet her. Noemi Del Toro was the embodiment of motherhood. An aura of love and peacefulness radiated around her in golden light. Even though her hair had grayed, it sparkled in the light as she entered through the arched opening. Still a beautiful woman, she moved gracefully but with purpose.

"Mom, I've been waiting for you."

"I would hope so." Her knowing green eyes lit

on him. "You've found her. Is she here?"

"No, Mom. She didn't come with me. She had business of her own to take care of. I just came back to take care of a few things."

"I'm glad you found her." She opened her arms to embrace him. "That other one has been snooping around."

"What do you mean snooping?" Mason asked Gabe over their mother's shoulder.

"She's come to the office a few times. She seems to think we need her for some reason. I told the assistant you hired to be nice, but not tell her anything." Gabe sat the tumbler down on an end table making the ice clink against the glass.

"Eva doesn't need to be there at all. It's over."

"She thinks since the TV idea was hers, she should be involved." Still holding onto Mason's hands his mother pulled him down to sit next to her on the loveseat.

"But it's over. I wouldn't dare try that again after the last mess."

"I agree. We don't need the bad publicity." Standing again, Gabriel paced.

"Gabe, who do you think set us up?" Mason had thought it through so many times, but still wasn't close to coming up with an answer.

"I don't know. Does it matter? It's over." His brother stopped to gaze out of the window into the luscious courtyard.

"If it's someone on our team, we need to know. It could ruin any credibility we have left, if they try it again."

The surprise on his face was genuine as he turned back to Mason. "Do you think they'd do it again? Why would someone on our team want to ruin us?"

"I can't answer that, but if it was someone else, someone not on our team, they'd be on the video. We know who was there."

"How? Did we have the video running the whole time?"

"Ben's very good at what he does. Recording everything is his business. He's meticulous when it comes to evidence."

"I can't imagine anyone on our team doing that. Who do you suspect?" Shaking his salt and pepper hair, Gabriel leaned against the back of the arm chair.

"I don't know but I need to figure it out." Mason knew if he had that piece of the puzzle, it would help heal things between him and Serena.

"Well, it certainly wasn't me."

"I never thought it was. You had no reason to sabotage our chances of getting a show."

"Who did Mason?" The worry on his mother's brow made him flinch. He hadn't meant to bother her with this business.

The investigator he had originally hired to find Serena, was now set to a different task.

"Mom, we all wanted the show."

"Was that why they did it, to make sure the show was picked up?"

"Well, if they did, they weren't too smart about it." Gabe pushed away from the chair to pace again.

"Exactly. It was meant to be found."

"Could it have been one of the TV crew?"

Mason shrugged. "Yes, that was my first thought, but why? What stake would they have in it?"

"You're not thinking it was Serena?" His mother

could always read him.

He hung his head shamefully. "When she left so abruptly what was I to think?"

"Mason. She left because you accused her." His brother's voice, now irritated, spoke the truth and he knew it.

"What?" Shocked, his mother sat up straighter.

"It didn't come out right. You know how I get. Believe me, I'm still paying for it." Running a hand through his hair, he thought again of the hurt on Serena's face.

"You have to fix that."

"I know Mom."

"For what it's worth, I don't think it was her. She's like you. There's no need to fake it." Gabe began pacing again as he considered the suspects. "My money's on somebody outside the team. Maybe paid off by one of the other teams being considered for a show. I wouldn't put it past Graham Young or one of his Sentinel crew."

"That's what I'm thinking, as well as Ben," Mason agreed, then added, "Once I was able to think rationally."

"So you'll go back to her then and make this right." His mother's voice was firm as she spoke. It wasn't a question or a request, but an order.

"I'm going to try, Mom."

"You will. You belong together."

He nodded in agreement. If only he could convince Serena of that.

CHAPTER 16

Serena stole quick glances at the moving map location dot on her phone while minding the traffic around her. Slowing down before the dot arrived at the destination, she put her phone down. The owner had told her over the phone that finding the bridal shop would be easy. The old Victorian home looked oddly out of place in the middle of the busy downtown bustle. Serena couldn't help but smile at the perfectness of it. Pulling into the small parking lot, she relaxed. This was going to work out.

Wedded Bliss was a quaint and quirky mix of old and new wedding retailery with a fairytale feel. The owner knew her stuff. Brides would be excited simply to cross that threshold into a whimsical world of white in the hopes of finding the perfect dress.

This meeting could have waited, but she knew everyone would want to know where she had been. Adding this meeting to her trip was her way of covering herself. Wedding business. It wouldn't be a lie, not totally. Not that it mattered anymore, that particular cat was out of the bag. Faith and Claire wouldn't care, but Mason... He wouldn't understand. She knew she shouldn't care, but she did. Their shared memories of a past life together had created a bond. She loved him, and she didn't want to hurt him even if they didn't end up together.

As she reached the picturesque porch, complete with spindle railings, Serena tried to push Mason from her mind. She had a mission to accomplish. This was important. The door creaked on its hinges, as she pushed it opened. She stepped in, taking a moment to let the shop's ambiance wash over her, she let the door close behind her. Instantly aware of the memories and emotions still hovering, she let her eyes adjust. The scented candles and the smell of fabric couldn't completely mask the aroma of musty oldness.

"Hi! Can I help you?" A bright cheery voice resonated from a rack of pastel colored bridesmaid dresses.

"Yes. I'm here to see Michelle LeBert."

"Oh, yeah. You must be Mrs. Del Toro." The rack shook a bit before a dark haired woman stepped from behind it. Her shiny straight black hair hung sleekly past her shoulders as she straightened to greet Serena. Suddenly uncomfortable with Mason's last name, she wondered why she had ever taken it.

"Umm, please call me Serena." She offered her hand in greeting, trying to shake the image of herself in a white lace gown.

"Nice to meet you. I'm Michelle. I have to say, after we talked on the phone, I'm so excited about this. I try to offer that here. You know, individual service. Private sessions where the bride can take her time and try on as many dresses as she wants. No fighting over racks." The last sentence was emphasized with an eye roll and a friendly grin.

"Right. I want the same thing. It would just be an extension of the service you already provide. Your service, my place. I would love to offer that as part of the package of getting married at Coeur du Bayou."

"I'm game." The bright smile Michelle offered was guarded but genuine. Serena felt an instant bond. She recognized a kindred spirit. An entrepreneur making a place for herself where she didn't fit in. The same charm of the old home in the midst of the new modern buildings. Michelle had the same appeal. She didn't belong in the city, her accent brought visions of country sunsets and the smell of wildflowers.

"Just like that?"

"Yeah. I mean we have to work out details, but I'm willing to give it a try. I really want to see this house, too. Come on. Let's go to my office. My next bride doesn't come in till four."

Serena followed her through a maze of white covered in plastic.

"You want to look?" Michelle looked back over her shoulder with a mischievous grin.

"Yeah, I do but let's talk first." Running her hand over a plastic covering, she admired the dress underneath. A prickling feeling on the back of her neck made her pause. "Michelle, are you married?"

"Well, that's not awkward." The frown on her face told of disappointment and regret.

"I'm sorry. I just got this feeling."

"Like what?" Narrowing her eyes, she placed a hand on her hip obviously expecting to be offended.

"I think you're going to meet someone."

"Who?" Eyes widening in surprise, Michelle's hand dropped lifelessly to her side.

"I don't know."

"If you get a name and address let me know. Hell, just the name. I can track him down." Laughing, she turned back towards her office.

"I'm sorry. That was weird. I normally keep stuff like that to myself."

"Hey, if you've got some magic that marries people off, our new arrangement is going to be successful."

***

After going over financial and practical details, Serena showed Michelle pictures from Claire's engagement party. Eager to show off the house and her hard work, Serena felt Ben's photos captured the feel of what she was trying to accomplish. Michelle's appreciation of the details were vocalized with generous variations of wows and ahhs. While admired the photos, Serena flipped through catalogs, marking styles of dresses she thought Claire would like. Several reminded her of Faith, so she tagged those, too. Remembering the dream, she shivered.

"Wow! Your house is amazing."

"Thanks. I've worked really hard for this." Serena

couldn't help the burst of pride she felt, having done as much of the work as she could herself.

"These pictures are great. You'll have to give me the photographer's name."

"Ben. Ben Peltier." The afternoon light from the window shone on the catalog pages as she flipped slowly through.

"I'm guessing all of these guys are taken. So, not my mystery man?" Michelle looked up from her desk with another eye roll.

Serena laughed, leaning over the desk to point out Claire and Evan. "This is the happy couple." Then finding a picture of Faith and Jake, she continued, "This is Faith and Jake. I'm sure we'll be planning their wedding next. Faith made the cake. Did you see it?"

"Wow, if she does work like that I might be able to send her some business, too." Michelle flipped back to the picture of the cake to take a second look.

"Well, it might be a little far, but who knows what could happen?" Serena sat back into the sunbeam resuming her search.

Michelle continued to flip through the pictures, stopping every now and then to take a closer look.

"What's this?" Holding a picture close to her face, Michelle studied it intently then looked to Serena. "What is that?"

"Let me see."

She held out the picture of Claire standing at the top of the stairs, clearly upset. The shadowy figure of a man loomed behind her.

"Damn it, Ben," Serena muttered to herself, taking the photo from Michelle. "It's nothing. He wasn't supposed to put that in there."

"Wait a minute." Michelle snatched the picture back to look again. "Is that a person?"

"It's just a shadow, really. The photographer was trying to be funny."

"No, that's not a joke. Your house is haunted too? Now I really want to see it for myself."

Serena nodded silently. Michelle was obviously not a stranger to the paranormal. The sensations she felt upon entering were confirmed. Michelle's shop had its own presence, and Michelle wasn't afraid. She would fit in great at Coeur du Bayou.

"So, how soon are we planning to have the first dress appointment with the bride?" Pushing the pictures aside, Michelle ran her finger over the desk planner considering dates.

No, she didn't frighten easy. That was a good thing.

"As soon as you have the dresses in the sizes I've marked."

"That's some very different styles… And sizes." Michelle raised an eyebrow at Serena.

"They're not all for her."

Richie be damned. This was going to happen.

CHAPTER 17

There was something going on. Serena could feel it. She had been back over a week, and everything was quiet; too quiet. Even the spirits were silent. She felt nothing from Richie or Anna.

Her friends had also been scarce. Faith had been limiting her time to just baking then hurrying out the door as soon as the baked goods were cool enough to transport. Claire was staying away like Evan had requested. Ben worked quietly around her, watching the readings, changing out memory cards and batteries. Serena often forgot he was in the house. On the other hand, Mason had yet to return and she felt his absence the most.

If she were to be honest with herself, she would have to admit her disappointment that he wasn't waiting for her when she returned. With each passing day her disappointment grew and so did the longing. Her time with Mason had been the happiest she could ever remember. She had been herself with him, no hiding. Until he had accused her. The betrayal had been more than she could bear.

"Hey, Rena." Ben poked his head through the opening of the bookcase door.

"Yeah?" She looked up from the open catalogs on her desk she had been staring at for the last hour.

"I was wondering if you've heard from Mason."

"No. Why?"

"I figured he'd be back by now." Absently playing with the door latch, his eyes wondered over the catalogs on her desk.

"Is something wrong?"

"No, not really. I just had some audio I wanted a second opinion on." Ben hovered awkwardly in the doorway. He took a step into her office, then took a step back.

"I can do it," Serena offered brightly waving him inside her office.

"Sure. When you have time." His blue eyes darted toward the doorway before his body turned away.

"Ben, did anything happen while I was away?"

Hesitating a moment too long, Ben slowly turned towards her.

"No, not really. Door slammed one night, but nothing else." He shrugged, not looking into her eyes.

"Mmm..." She considered, nodding at him. "No crying?"

"Maybe. There could have been." He scratched his head as if trying to recall.

"So Faith was here?"

"What?" he asked wide eyed, then cast his gaze downwards. "I don't remember."

"Ben, don't lie. You know exactly everything that happens here. It's recorded somewhere."

"Ok, yes." Finally making his way into her office, Ben sat heavily on an antique chair. "She had some baking to do and snuck in the kitchen. I told her she shouldn't be here, but she wouldn't listen."

In his eagerness to explain himself, he leaned forward. His frustrated expression reminded her of a child wrongly accused lamenting over the injustice of it all.

"It's ok. I gave her a key."

"Oh, so you're not mad?" Ben sat up curiously, the rickety chair groaned in protest.

"No, I knew she'd probably come anyway." Serena laughed. "She's safe here. Anna wouldn't let anything happen to her."

"Oh, then why did you make such a fuss?" Leaning back in the small wooden chair, he breathed a sigh of relief.

"Well, it was worth a try. I figured it would give everyone time to calm down."

"Yeah, I think it did." Stretching out he clasped his hands behind his head, the wood spindles underneath him squeaked with his shifting weight. "You and Mason needed some time, too."

Serena rolled her eyes at his attempt to change the subject, then gave in.

"Yes, we did. I think we'll be fine." Serena smiled thinking about his return.

Hearing a voice from the foyer, Ben called through the doorway, "In here."

"What's going on?" Evan's large form filled the opening. His tone made the question more of an accusation.

"Evan. What now?" Feeling his dark mood, Serena stood.

"I found this in the party pictures." He eyed Ben with a dark look as he handed Serena the picture of Richie's ghostly form standing behind Claire on the staircase.

"Ben…," Serena hissed.

"Wait a minute. Serena, I gave you that picture. Remember, you left it in the kitchen?" Holding his hands up in front of himself, Ben didn't try to stand with Evan looming so close.

"Maybe Faith picked it up by accident," Serena offered the most logical explanation. Evan's face remained unconvinced. "Look, I'm sorry. It wasn't supposed to be in there."

"Anything else happen?" His black eyes narrowed on Serena.

"No. It's been really quiet." Looking to Ben for confirmation, she waited for his nod then asked, "Why?"

"Something's going on." Hands on his hips, Evan towered over her, only the desk between them.

"What do you mean?" Her earlier suspicions nagged at her. Holding her breath, Serena waited for his answer.

"Claire's acting funny."

"Don't worry about it, Evan. I'm sure it's just the wedding stuff. She's excited. We all are." She sat back at her desk, trying to reassure the brooding deputy.

"Yeah."

"What's the matter? You don't sound excited," Ben asked cautiously.

"She's hell bent on getting married here." Evan shook his head miserably leaning against the door frame.

"Evan, it's going to be fine. You just leave all the details to us. All you have to do is show up and say I do."

"Yeah, I will. I just don't think I'm being unreasonable."

"Did Claire say that?"

"Uh, huh. Faith used other words."

"I can imagine." Ben chuckled.

"She called me unreasonable. You know what she said? If we can't get married in the house, she wants to get married in the graveyard."

Serena had to bite her lip to keep from laughing at his horrified expression. It was clever. She'd have to ask whose idea it was, Faith's or Claire's.

"So, it's back at the house then?" She didn't even try to hide her smile.

"Yeah, well, we talked about having it out on the lawn if the weather's good. If not, then inside."

"Inside it is then."

"If the weather's bad…" catching her meaning, Evan gave her a smirk. "Ha. Very funny."

"What?" Ben asked.

"When Claire and Evan have a big event there's always a chance of rain. Or flood," she teased.

"Oh, yeah. It was raining the night of the party."

At Evan's grumble, Serena tried to put his mind at ease. "Look, we'll make provisions for both. Just in case, ok?"

"So if it's outside we shouldn't have to worry about the spooky stuff, right?"

"I think so. Please don't worry."

He nodded then sighed. "So what's going on with my sister?"

"Shouldn't you ask her?" Surprised at the questioning, she wondered again what had happened while she was away.

"I just meant with the ghost stuff. She hasn't been talking about it much."

"Probably because of the kids."

"Yeah, I guess so. Jake seems to be pretty freaked out, too." Hands in his pockets now, Evan glanced casually around at the purple walls of her room.

"Oh. I haven't seen him in a while so I don't know."

"Y'all haven't gotten anywhere with that? All the video stuff." Directed at Ben, Evan's tone was still casual but his expression was serious.

"We did get a name. Anna." Ben glanced nervously at Serena, obviously unsure of how much he should say.

"Damn. I shouldn't have asked." Evan rubbed a hand over his eyes.

"Then why did you?"

"Because I get the feeling something's going on or something happened. Those two..," he paused to point at Serena, "and you, are always up to something."

Serena laughed at his accusation even as her suspicions grew. "I assure you. I'm not up to anything."

"Ok." Evan nodded at her unconvincingly.

"Except for planning the wedding." Holding up a catalog for emphasis, she gave Evan an innocent look.

"But if there's something I need to know you'll tell me, right?"

"Absolutely." She gave him her most reassuring smile.

"Alright, thanks."

After Evan made his way back through the open door, Ben gave her a questioning look. "You'd really tell him?"

"He said if there's something he needed to know," she purred at Ben, handing him a catalog. "Now, help me find a dress?"

"For what?"

"Bridesmaid dresses. Faith, Elle and me."

"Y'all have the same coloring and probably are close to the same size." He considered, flipping through the catalog intently.

Surprised at his willingness to help, she arched an eyebrow. Ben, always watching and gathering information, knew more than he let on. That picture had popped up not once, but twice. Did he leave it there on purpose?

Her next line of thinking brought her to the question she hated to ask herself. Could he have been the one to sabotage their chance at the ghost hunting show? Why would he? It just didn't fit.

She studied him as he searched the catalog. He was pleasant looking, not hard on the eyes at all. His personality was charming and his timing with a wisecrack was impeccable. No, she sensed no malice or underlying anger. More importantly, he had wanted the TV show more than anyone else. Capturing evidence of real hauntings, ghosts and paranormal activity drove him.

"This one." His blue eyes shone with excitement as he pointed to a picture of a dress. "This one would look amazing on Elle. I mean, y'all."

"Wow! I love it, Ben. And I think you're right." She was still smiling at the slip of Elle's name when she heard the front door open.

"We're in here," she called wondering if Evan had come back. Then she felt him.

"Mason." Her hand shook slightly, just a tremor. The real quaking was in her core. Her eyes hungrily watched the doorway for his appearance.

"You guys just amaze me." Ben stood to shake Mason's hand as he strode through the open book case.

"What have I done now?" Mason flashed a smile, offering his hand in greeting.

"Hey man. Nothing. Just that thing you guys do when you know the other one is around."

"Rena." His voice was warm as Mason made his way around the desk to plant a kiss on her forehead.

"Mason." She grabbed his hand before he could retreat. "I'm glad you're back."

Ben grinned at them. "I'll let you two catch up. I've got some stuff I need to check on."

"Ok." Mason chuckled and squeezed her hand as Ben hurried from the room. "Was that the deputy leaving?"

"Yeah."

"Everything ok?"

"Yeah." She got up from the desk to close the door.

"Wow. You are happy to see me."

"I am, but I think something's going on." Serena leaned back on the closed door, wrestling with telling Mason of her suspicions about Ben.

"There could be." Walking towards her slowly, his green gold eyes burned over her body.

"No, that's why Evan was here. Something's going on. I just don't know what."

"With Ben or Evan?" He paused slightly before reaching for her.

"Evan says Claire and Faith are acting funny."

Mason stopped her with a kiss so hot and searing it wiped all thought from her mind. The quaking at her core rumbled. Breaking the kiss, he whispered in her ear. "I've missed you, love."

Closing her eyes, she whispered his name. It was a plea for release.

He pressed his forehead to hers with a sigh. "You're driving me crazy. I told myself I wouldn't do this, but I can't help myself. Rena." His strong hands were at her waist, squeezing gently.

In answer, she slid her leg up his, wrapping it around his waist and pulled him towards her. Their bodies melding together in the heat of the moment. A groan escaped her lips as she felt his hardness against her.

"We are bound," she whispered, and surrendered.

CHAPTER 18

"So tell me what you think is going on." Mason's husky voice brought her gently back to herself. Sunlight streamed through the window of her office highlighting bits of dust floating through the air. Lying next to Mason on the daybed, Serena felt perfectly complete in this moment.

"Mmmm.... I think something happened while we were away." Snuggling closer to Mason, she laid her head on his shoulder, content.

"To Ben?"

"Ben admitted Faith was here. Evan came by because Claire has been acting funny, too." Suddenly tired, she stifled a yawn.

"You think they tried a session or something?" Mason's concern was apparent as his arm tightened around her. Then he answered his own question. "No, Ben wouldn't attempt that."

"No," Serena agreed but the nagging thought of the picture that kept popping up made her not so sure of anything.

"What?"

"It's just that where this house is concerned, I can't see. I feel like I'm missing something so obvious." She ran a hand down his bare chest. Mason grabbed it, holding it over his still pounding heart.

"Love, you know I'll do whatever it takes to help work this out. I know how important this is to you, so it's important to me. I'll stay as long as you need me to, but I warn you. My mother is expecting to see you soon. I wouldn't be surprised if she shows up here."

"Your mother?"

"Oh, yes. She wanted to know why I hadn't brought you home with me."

"You went home?" The words made her homesick for a place she knew no longer existed. Her grandmother had been gone for years. Mason's family had been the closest she felt to a home, until Coeur du Bayou.

"I had some things to take care of and I hadn't exactly told anyone where I was going. I told her you were busy planning a wedding. She said you'd make a beautiful bride. Of course, I agreed." He brought her hand to his lips, kissing it lightly.

"Mason." She tried to pull her hand away, but he held it to him.

"I know there are things we need to work out, but I won't entertain the idea of you and I not being together."

"Let's not get into that now, ok?"

"Fair enough. I need to learn when to keep my mouth shut."

"Yes, you do." Leaning up, she kissed him on that mouth before climbing out of the daybed.

It was magic. It had to be. She felt his eyes on her as she pulled the sundress over her head and wiggled it down over her hips. Would the magic fade? Or would it be strong enough to endure their emotional tug of war?

"I'm not going anywhere, Rena." His husky voice washed away the creeping doubts. "Where did you go?"

"Hmm. Oh, wedding stuff."

Mason nodded, watching her intently. "Have you made any progress on that?"

"Yes, I think Evan is softening to the idea. He'd rather it out on the lawn, but we'll plan for both."

"We should do another session." Mason suggested, stretching lazily as he watched her slip her panties on under the dress.

"First, I'd like to find out what we missed."

"If Ben knows, I'll find out. What about Richie?"

Her muscles tightened at the mention of his name. He'd been oddly quiet which made her suspicious.

"Nothing since I've been home. Why? Do you feel something?" Folding a leg under herself, Serena sat on the edge of the bed anxious for his answer. Mason closed his eyes and breathed in deeply.

"Not in here."

Relieved, she drank in the sight of him. Sunlight danced across his bare chest giving his tanned skin a warm glow.

"Are you afraid of him Rena?" he asked softly.

"I can't let myself be." The memory of Richie pushing a battered Claire through her door last Halloween made her angry.

"I wish I would have been here for you. He could have hurt you." Mason rubbed a hand over her thigh.

Feeling his unease, she threaded her fingers through his to reassure him. "He didn't."

"But he's still here. Isn't he?"

"I don't know. The house warns me. I wasn't sure at first, but it does. It doesn't want him here, that much I know."

"The house or Anna?"

"I don't know. It feels like the house to me, but it could be her. She's not very clear to me for some reason. You feel her, right?"

"Mmm, yes. A definite female presence. A lot of sadness."

"What else?"

"Well, the very angry male figure of course. That one was hard to miss." Serena felt a shiver pass through him. "The burnt smell. I'm not sure which one it's connected to yet."

"Mason." Her heart felt heavy and her eyes watered, remembering a time when they were open and honest with each other. Could it be that way again?

"What is it?"

"I don't want you hurt."

"Worried about me?" He squeezed her hand with a smile.

"Yes, you know that. I just can't see this."

"We're going to figure it out. I won't leave you again until this is..."

"Shh..." Leaning forward she kissed him softly. "No promises."

Mason pulled away and looked into her eyes, a flash of pain and loneliness crossing his face. "No. We can fix this. It can be different."

He reached for her again, his fingertips brushing the material of her dress as she rose gracefully from the bed. Serena wandered over to sit at her desk. She wanted it to be the way it was before. So much uncertainty surrounded them, she couldn't see her way out of it.

The daybed groaned as Mason sat up.

"You'll see." He didn't look at her as he dressed himself, his jaw set in a determined line.

"What are you up to?"

"I'm going to fix this and I'm going to start by finding out what Ben knows." Finally looking at her, he held out a hand. "You coming?"

<hr />

They found Ben in his room engrossed in his work. Looking up at them in surprise over his laptop, he asked cautiously, "Hey, you guys ok?"

"Yeah, we're good." Mason gave him a devilish smile then got right to the point. "Something happened with Faith while we were gone."

"Yeah," Ben rolled his eyes. "She came to bake. And yeah..."

"You recorded it?"

"Of course. You know, after it was over. I couldn't see what she did."

"So you were with her when it happened?" Serena raised an eyebrow.

"Yeah, when I realized she was here I figured I better keep an eye on her." He gulped loudly then began searching nervously for the file on his computer. "I think it's this one."

Ben clicked the mouse, and Faith's excited voice came from the speaker.

"*The rocker. He made the rocker for her and the baby. He knew she was pregnant. He wanted to marry her, to ask for her hand. Her father was away on business. Something about a gambling boat, I don't know. She was happy about the baby, but terrified of what her father would do if he found out. She spends a lot of time at the graveyard.*" Faith's voice drifted off.

"*No name?*" Ben asked.

"*I can't remember. I know it. I can feel it when it's happening.*"

"*What did she show you?*"

"*The room upstairs. Jake brought the rocker up for me. I sat by the window, rocking.*"

"Jake?" Claire's voice was filled with awe.

Ben fumbled with the mouse to click it off, a little too late.

"Claire was here?" Shocked, Serena's voice vibrated through the room. That explained the feeling she had, but she knew there was more.

"Yeah, I should have told you. She just showed up. Seriously you have some hard headed friends." Ben's eyes never left the computer screen.

"You're lucky no one else showed up. Or did they?" Leaning on the desk to get his attention, Serena asked through clenched teeth.

"No." Ben looked up at her. "Just Claire and

Faith. I told them they shouldn't be here."

"What did Claire want?"

"To pay me for the pictures, but I told her you had already." Shaking his head, he looked away again.

"Did you give her that picture?" Pointing her finger in Ben's face, Serena could feel her blood pressure rising.

"What picture?" Mason asked curiously.

"No, I told you. I gave it to you," Ben, now indignant, snapped back.

"What picture?" Mason asked again more forcefully.

"Show him. I'm sure you have another copy. They seem to be popping up all over." Waving her hands in the air for emphasis then crossing her arms, she turned towards the door angrily.

Ben dug through his folders, and handed Mason a picture.

"Is this what y'all saw?" Mason didn't shock easily, but Serena could hear the dismay in his voice.

"Yes."

"Incredible." Mason gasped. "Not enhanced?"

"No, that's the original." Ben's excitement was clear as he answered Mason.

"What happened with Claire?" Serena narrowed her eyes on Ben.

"What do you mean?"

"You wouldn't have kept the incident with Faith a secret, unless something else happened with Claire. You didn't want me to know Claire was here."

"Ok." Dragging his hand over his face, Ben sighed heavily. "Look, they wanted to help. Claire thought she might be able to talk to Richie. I was going to let Mason listen first. I didn't know if I should even tell you about it."

"Let Mason listen first?" she repeated furiously. "This is my house."

"Calm down, please."

"No, I won't, Reuben. I want to hear it."

"Rena, it's not pretty and I don't know that you'd want to."

"Ben, did Faith and Claire hear it?" Mason stepped in between them.

"No way. After Faith's episode they were pretty shook up. They haven't even asked about it. I'm glad because they don't need to hear it. It scared me. They would never come back."

"It scared you?" Mason asked surprised. Then pointed to the computer. "Play it."

Ben gave an uncertain glance in Serena's direction.

"Play it," she ordered.

"Ok, but…," Ben started to argue.

"Just play it," Mason said firmly, placing a hand on his shoulder.

Ben clicked the mouse a few more times, then his voice came from the speaker.

"*This is Ben Peltier here with Faith….*"

"*Faith Williams.*"

"*Claire Hebert.*"

"*Claire will be asking questions. Claire whenever you are ready.*"

A hiss escaped Serena's lips. "You let her ask questions?"

"Rena." Mason put a hand on her arm, then turned to Ben. "Why?"

"She wanted to. It was her idea. Faith jumped on the bandwagon and there was no talking her out of it.

Just listen... If you want," he added lamely.

"*Richie are you here?*" Claire sounded scared. A short silence followed.

"*Richie, it's Claire. We don't have your money. The police took it.*"

"*Questions, Claire, remember?*" Ben's voice was soft but clear.

"*Oh yeah,*" Claire answered, then in a louder voice, "*Richie, why are you here?*"

Through the hum of the electronics a hateful voice hissed, "*Stupid bitch!*"

"*Richie, what do you want?*"

"*My money... Bitch stole my money.*"

After a minute of silence, Claire spoke again. "*I guess I should have written some questions down.*"

"*Maybe you should ask him what hell feels like,*" Faith's voice dripped with sarcasm.

"*I know you came here because of the money, right?*" Claire continued. "*Did you ever love me?*"

"*No, no, no.*"

"*Claire.*" Ben's whisper almost covered the voice.

"*I just wondered. I think I know the answer, but I can't help thinking there was some good in there somewhere. Even if just at the beginning.*"

"*Never loved you, so stupid.*"

"*Richie, do you know I'm getting married? I'm so happy. For once I'm actually happy and you are not going to ruin this for me. You need to go!*" Claire's last statement was shouted into the recorder.

"*Gut you and your friend like a pig, cunt!*" The voice exploded from the speaker.

"*Ok, Claire. That's good.*" Ben's voice was calm, but firm. "*Faith give me the meter. You two should go. I'll pick this up.*"

"*Never leave. You can't leave.*" The voice hissed angrily.

"*Oh. Do you think we got something?*" Claire's voice was unsure.

"*I won't know until I go back through it. Besides the EMF meter going off, there's no evidence. But...*" Ben's voice was interrupted by a slamming door. "*Oh, man. Y'all need to go!*"

"*Faith!*" Claire cried out in fear.

"*Oh, shit, Faith,*" Ben's voice whispered.

Heavy footsteps sounded followed by a different voice screaming, "*No, Poppa. No!*"

The moaning and wailing that followed sent chills down Serena's spine. She reached over to click the mouse. "What did you need a second opinion on? Telling me?"

"I just thought maybe Mace should hear it first. I didn't know if you'd want to hear it."

Serena at a loss for words turned to Mason, who stared stone-faced at the laptop. "He won't hurt you or anybody else. He can't."

"So that was Richie?" Ben asked.

"Yes, it's him alright. Just as charming in death as he was when he was alive." Her jaw clenched in anger. This could ruin everything. "No one else heard this, right?"

"No, I told you. This is crazy. If they hear this, they would never come back."

"Erase it," Serena demanded.

"What?" Mason turned to her bewildered.

"No!" Ben shook his head.

"You left those pictures, Ben. I'm not going to have you mess this up."

"No one else will ever hear this, but I'm not

erasing it. This is evidence." He pulled the mouse protectively towards his body out of Serena's reach. "I didn't give Claire that picture. Faith must have picked it up."

"What about the one on my stack?"

"What about it? You saw it. What does that matter?" Ben shrugged over his desk.

"Those were to show potential clients and I showed them to a vender."

"Oh, sorry." Ben blinked, then frowned. "I thought you'd go through them first."

"So it wasn't on purpose?" Mason asked suspiciously, still looming over Ben's shoulder.

"Of course not." He eyed them both. "You two are made for each other."

"I won't argue with that, but this place....." Mason shook his head then turned to Serena. "I won't have you hurt or in danger."

"I'm not."

"It's never been so clear or so strong.... To catch an EVP like this combined with everything else going on here."

"Ah, you worried about me?" she asked turning his favorite question back on him.

"It's not a joke, Rena," Mason pleaded with her.

"Look guys, I'm sorry I didn't say anything before, but I did want a second opinion. Listen to the end again."

CHAPTER 19

Secrets. Serena hated them. Yet they seemed to be everywhere. Finding herself keeping a few of her own made her uncomfortable. She had tried to live her life as openly as possible.

Plans for the wedding were moving along. The day for the dress session had finally arrived. Nothing was going to stop her. This was the dream she had. It was about more than just one wedding. It was her future, with or without Mason. She found herself hoping more and more for 'with'.

He had stayed as promised. Dealing with business over emails and phone calls. They had settled into a comfortable routine and ended each day seeking each other out. She had taken to sleeping with him in his room after he complained about her small daybed.

Ben had stayed as well, doing what he did best, gathering information. Only leaving for a few photo sessions that had been booked months in advance.

Her thoughts turned to their ongoing investigation of the house. The sounds at the end of that recording where horrific, but supported her feeling that Anna was protecting them. Guarding the house.

The upside of secret keeping was that Claire and Faith seemed to be keeping their distance. Probably afraid to spill the beans about their secret session. Today they would all be here together.

Michelle was busy setting up racks of dresses in the big room. Serena had set up full length mirrors and screens for the dressing area.

Not wanting any distractions, she had tried unsuccessfully to get rid of Ben and Mason for the day. Ben had insisted on sticking around to take pictures. Once she considered it, she had to admit it would be a bonus for everyone involved. Claire would have keepsakes from the fitting. Michelle would have promotional pictures, and so would she. She knew Ben had used logic to diffuse any argument she had put up because he was nervous about this.

Richie had been quiet since the night of the EVP recording. She assumed it was too much to hope for that he had simply dissipated. Mason had been on edge since hearing the recording and refused to leave. Serena had grown used to his constant hovering. It felt natural.

Sounds from the kitchen made her smile. Faith

had shown up early to make refreshments for after the dresses were safely back in the plastic coverings. The smells brought Ben from his room. He lurked hopefully near the doorway, camera in hand.

Laughter from the porch alerted her to Claire and Elle's arrival. The house was as it should be, full of life and activity. It felt like a home. Her home. She opened the door to greet Elle and the bride to be.

Claire's excitement was obvious, as they continued their happy chatter. Claire had definitely found a home and family with the Bertrands. Serena smiled warmly as she greeted them.

"Hello, ladies. Are we ready to find the dress today?"

"Yes!" Claire squealed, her blue eyes shining with excitement. Her enthusiasm was contagious and spurred a whoop from Elle.

"Why don't you guys wait in the parlor until Michelle is ready with the dresses? I'll go find Faith." Serena left them to chatter and made her way to the kitchen. Ben hovered just outside the door sulking.

"What's wrong, Faith not letting you sample?" She laughed at him.

"What's Elle doing here?"

"She's in the wedding. The bridesmaids have to try on dresses, too."

"This is weird," Ben whispered more to himself, then frowned at her.

"You don't have to stay."

"No, I'm not going anywhere." He tapped the EMF meter hooked to his belt.

"Ugh. Do you have to do that today?"

"Yes," Mason spoke from behind her, "He does. If we have some warning like before maybe we can make sure no one else gets hurt."

"Ok, take some pictures of Claire and Elle waiting. Then go inside to catch their reaction when they see the dresses. Michelle should be ready soon. I'll get Faith."

The smells of the fresh baked cookies lured her into the warm, bright room. Faith stood at her sink scrubbing a baking pan. Her ponytail shook with each pass of her hand.

"Hey, you almost done in here?"

"Oh, yeah. Is it time?"

"They're all here in the parlor. I'd like a picture of you guys together before we start."

"Sure, but you should be in the picture, too."

"It's ok. I have things to see about, and you guys are family."

"You are too. You're in the wedding." Rinsing the pan, Faith gave her a perturbed look. "You need to be in the picture. We barely got any of you at the engagement party."

"It's not about me. Come on."

Faith wiped her hands with a dishrag, her brows furrowed. "Do you think something will happen?"

The question caught Serena off guard. Everyone had been avoiding all talk of anything paranormal.

"No, I don't. Everything's fine." She smiled widely at her friend. "Don't worry Faith. Let's just have some fun and think about the wedding."

"Yeah, ok."

Serena smiled. She was just a bit excited herself to try on the dresses. Wedding dresses. With her and Mason finally smoothing things out, she dared to hope for her own wedding one day. His mother had surprised her with a phone call, and an open invitation to visit her.

"You ok?"

"Yeah, I am. Let's go try on dresses."

———— ⟨⚬⚬⟩ ————

Mason watched the girls enter the big room. Amid the ooo's and ahh's, he caught a glimpse of Serena's face. God, she was a sight, but when she was truly happy, not guarded, it was a rare thing indeed. The brightness radiating from her floated around her in a soft haze of gold light. A rush of love flooded over him. He had been surprised to find her waiting for him when he returned. When he had reached for her, he knew she wouldn't turn him away. Since that day things were as they should be. They were together; a couple, partners. Days were spent working together, and nights resting in each other's arms. Not wanting to mess things up again, he kept a tight grip on his thoughts, and an even tighter one on his mouth.

Stepping in to help things go as smoothly as possible, he was determined to show Serena things could be as before. Being familiar with the hospitality industry, he knew some things, but weddings, not so much. Clearly over his head, with invitations and etiquette, he had watched over the process with interest. Seeing firsthand the work Serena had done to make this day special for her friend showed him that she did indeed belong here. This house was made for this and so was she. Serena had a knack for putting people at ease. She could create an atmosphere with a few simple items and her smile. Just as she danced with her soul, she had poured all of herself into this one day.

Ben quietly snapped pictures of the girls as they inspected the dresses. Michelle cast uneasy glances in Ben's direction, trying to dodge the camera. He was soon forgotten as Michelle showed Claire a dress and urged her to try it on. Leaving them to continue the search, Mason stepped into the foyer. Testing the air around him, he continued to wander through the downstairs rooms. It was quiet. Not entirely sure what he would do if something did happen, he was thankful for the quiet. Making his way back to the foyer, he stopped at the foot of the staircase. He sighed with relief when he still felt nothing. He stayed alert, remembering the sounds on the audio. He couldn't see everything, hear everything, or feel everything. Things could be happening around him, and he'd never be the wiser. Mason knew without a doubt if the others heard that audio, they'd never come back. It was better that they couldn't hear or feel these things.

Hearing a barrage of excited voices from the big room, Mason wandered back over to peek in the doorway. Claire stood before a mirror gazing dreamily at the dress she was wearing. Everyone flitted excitedly around her. Michelle tugged at the back explaining about the train. Ben snapped pictures as Faith held up Claire's hair to compare the merits of an updo to a half updo.

As Elle stepped from behind a screen, Mason caught Ben's appreciative expression in the mirror and grinned in agreement. The dreaded bridesmaids' dresses in this case were quite flattering. A wispy chiffon plum colored gown with a haltered neckline and a layered handkerchief hem skirt, made Elle even more fairy like.

"Oh, Ben, you were right. It's amazing on her!" Serena exclaimed before disappearing behind a screen.

Horrified, Ben nervously pressed buttons on the camera. "Umm, yeah. With y'alls' dark coloring I knew it would make a great picture."

"Well, you've got a good eye." Michelle smiled flirtatiously at him.

Elle turned to see herself in the mirror. Her lip curled as she turned sideways.

"What's the matter Elle? Don't you like it?" Claire asked disappointed.

"No, I love it!" Smiling at Claire in the mirror, Elle added with a grumble, "I'll have to dye my hair to match though."

"Oh, yeah," Faith snorted, "Brother dear will love that."

"Ben." Elle stomped her bare foot on the wood floor with a smack.

"Hmm?"

"Are you going to take my picture or not?" Huffing impatiently, she turned from the mirror to face him.

"Oh, yeah, sure." Ben held up the camera and Elle struck a pose.

"Faith, why don't you go put on your dress, too? Ben can get a picture of you guys together," Michelle suggested.

Mason assumed Serena was putting on the same dress and waited with anticipation. The dress would be just as stunning on Serena with her dark curls. Faith found her dress and disappeared behind another screen. Moments later, Serena stepped out from behind the screen making the room still. Mason's knees wanted to buckle. He grabbed the door for support. The white lace gown clung to her dancer's body and sprouted a full skirt well below her hips. The delicate lace flowed off of her tanned shoulders into billowy sleeves.

"Wow! Rena!" Ben frantically snapped the camera in her direction. Serena smiled, then swiveling her hips she turned to look over her shoulder at Ben. The back of her dress, simply wasn't there. Her bronzed back was bare to the waist, and the lace clung deliciously to her back side before the gathered folds of the skirt.

Claire made a strangled moan before protesting, "No! Mason you shouldn't be here. It's bad luck!"

"Claire," Serena laughed. "It's your wedding, not mine. I just fell in love with this dress. I couldn't help myself."

"It's gorgeous on you!" Michelle grinned, then turned to Mason. "I didn't know you guys were engaged too."

"We're not." Serena looked down at the dress, smoothing it gently with her hands.

Unable to find his voice, Mason just stared at her still gripping the door. Concerned, Serena hurried towards him whispering, "What's wrong?"

"I'm her husband!" His words echoed in the big room. Everyone froze, sharing a tense beat, unsure of what was happening.

"I'm fine. It's gorgeous, love," he whispered hoarsely to Serena, then slid the door closed.

Oh god, he remembered. No, no. It couldn't be. Trembling, he made his way to the parlor, grabbing onto a chair back for support. The memories came flooding back. Her and him, as always. They were bound. Their love burned and consumed him. She danced before him in a white dress, her face radiated love and happiness. Dancing. She was always dancing. Then there was someone else in the dark with her. Dancing with her. The jealousy and anger made him unclear. Everything was a haze of red. She was crying and pleading, but it was lost in the roaring of his mind. Blood on the dress soaked through the lace, dying it a perfect shade of crimson. He had held her, howling like an animal. Darkness swirled as the pain engulfed him. He had killed the only thing he ever loved.

It made sense now. Why he had searched for her. Dreamed of her. He was still howling on the inside. It also explained the jealousy and mistrust. He had to fix this. This time he would.

Confused at Mason's reaction, Serena stared at the door he had shut in her face. She could feel his pain, but didn't understand what had happened. Turning to Ben, she gave him a questioning look. He looked down at the meter then shrugged helplessly.

"You guys go ahead. I'll be right back." She gave them a smile before slipping through the door to find Mason. Standing in the parlor, his back was towards her, head hanging and his hands gripping the chair back.

"Mace, what's wrong?" she whispered softly.

He turned toward her, his eyes glistened with unshed tears. "Mi Amor."

Serena reached for him, but he held out a hand to stop her.

"Take the dress off please. I can't stand it." His voice broke, as he closed his eyes against the threatening tears.

Pulling her hand back, the rejection burned. "What?" she hissed.

"I'll be upstairs, if you need me." Walking from the room briskly, he left her standing alone wondering if the magic had finally faded.

CHAPTER 20

His first instinct was to run. Just get away. The long buried memory, now uncovered, wouldn't leave him. When he was able to sleep, he'd wake in a panic after reliving the rage and horror of his blood soaked hands holding her lifeless body. Most nights Mason would just hold Serena, feeling her breath move through her until he fell asleep. Some nights sleep wouldn't come at all. He knew there was nowhere to run from this. The memories would be with him forever.

Hearing laughter from the kitchen, Mason made his way down the service stairs. Serena must not remember. Of course she had been fearless until those last moments. The doubts crept in. Maybe she was right. Maybe their lesson was to live without each other. He didn't want to think about that.

Another thought crept in. Was his rage the connection to this place? To Richie and the father?

He couldn't voice these concerns out loud. If Serena didn't recall the trauma of her death in that past life, he wouldn't be the one to tell her. Their shared memories of passion were all he wanted her to remember. Not the fear, the rage, or the everlasting guilt he felt.

Mason entered the kitchen to Ben's voice, sounding appalled, he asked, "What are you talking about?"

"You gave Michelle your number. I heard you," Faith teased.

"Faith, that was business. Michelle liked his pictures." Serena wiggled her eyebrows over her coffee cup. Her laughter, joined by Faith's, filled the kitchen.

"Geesh, if this is what having a sister is like you can keep it. Don't you have your own siblings to torture?"

"Umm, no I don't." Serena smiled at him.

"Speaking of my siblings, what was the crack about Elle wanting to go see Gil?" Faith raised an eyebrow at Ben.

"I don't know what you're talking about." Ben put a forkful of food in his mouth, then noticed Mason standing in the doorway.

Following his gaze, Faith asked, "Coffee?"

"Yeah, but I'll get it. Don't get up." He gave her a halfhearted smile as he shuffled to the coffee pot. "I think this is the first time I've ever seen you actually sitting in this room."

Serena watched him with concern as he poured the coffee. "Still not sleeping, hun?"

"Got a few hours." He looked around the room. "What's next?"

"Well, we did the dress thing without any trouble, right?" Faith asked hopefully.

"Yeah, I didn't notice anything," Ben shook his head and continued, "and nothing else has happened. It's been days."

"I didn't feel anything." Serena's eyes never left Mason's. "Did you?"

He had been avoiding this conversation for days. "No, I didn't feel Richie at all. Maybe he's gone." Mason gave Faith a reassuring smile and leaned against the counter next to Serena.

"Ok, great. So, another session with me then?"

"Uh, yeah, if you're up to it." Ben looked to Mason for confirmation.

Mason nodded silently, taking a cautious sip of his coffee.

"Good, we can find out more. I know the name will come out soon. I can feel it." Faith's dark eyes shone with enthusiasm as she leaned on the counter in front of her.

"The name?" Mason asked absently.

"Yeah, the guy…" Faith stopped suddenly, looking into the empty cup before her.

"He made her the rocker because he knew she was pregnant, and he planned to marry her. Was there anything else we need to know?" Serena asked patiently slipping an arm around Mason's waist.

"Umm…" Faith's enthusiasm dimmed as she looked to Ben.

"I had to tell them. It happened and they needed to know."

"So Claire talking to Richie, it worked?" Faith asked hopefully. "We were wondering."

"We don't know. Maybe. He's been quiet." Serena smiled. "Let's just concentrate on Anna."

"Let's do it." Pulling off her apron, Faith stood to hang it on the peg near the back door.

"Now?" Ben choked.

"Yes, she's right. The sooner we get to the bottom of this the better." Mason could feel Serena's eyes on him as he stepped away from her. "You'll be able to move on with your plans, Rena."

Unable to meet her eyes, he took his coffee and left them in the kitchen to prepare.

Serena watched them set up in the pale yellow room. It was hard to be a calm observer when you cared so deeply for the people involved. Ben was busy checking the equipment and Faith laid back on the bed without having to be told. Mason, when he finally joined them, looked exhausted. The dark circles under his eyes were worrying her.

Ever since the dress session, he had not been sleeping. The first night, when he hadn't sought her out at bedtime, she had found him pacing in his room. He told her it wasn't Richie, and she believed him. The house hadn't warned her and she had felt nothing out of the ordinary. Their routine stayed the same, but something was bothering him. Each night she'd fall asleep in his arms only to find him watching her when she awoke.

Now he took his seat next to the bed, giving her a smile that didn't reach his eyes. "Are we ready?"

Ben nodded and Faith closed her eyes instead of answering.

"Faith, concentrate on your breathing. Inhale, exhale. Relax and remember you are safe. When it's time to end the session, I'll say the word j'adoube. When I say the word j'adoube, you will awaken immediately refreshed and energized." Mason's voice was smooth and soothing. After a few minutes, he spoke again. "Anna, are you with us?"

"Yes." A soft giggle followed.

"Does your father know about the baby?"

"No, not yet. He won't be pleased. He wanted me to marry Harold."

"Who is Harold?"

"The son of one of his business associates. Poppa says they're building a town here and it's very important."

"I don't understand. What's important Anna?"

"That I marry Harold. His father will probably be mayor, and Poppa needs to be on the town council. So they can bring the gambling boat."

"I thought your father owned the lumber yard."

"Yes, he does but he's trying to help build the town."

"Oh." Mason looked confused, then continued on another course of questioning. "Do you like Harold?"

"No. He sweats a lot." Her nose wrinkled distastefully.

"But you love someone else?"

"Yes, we're going to have a baby." Joy and shame played across her face. Her hands moved over her stomach making circular motions.

"What's his name, Anna?"

"Poppa doesn't like him because he's from across the river, but I don't care. I only stayed to take care of Momma, but she's gone. I want to go live with him, but he says we have to wait until Poppa gives his blessing. Poppa won't. I know he won't."

"Will you see him again soon?"

"Poppa's away again. He'll come tonight after Cook's to bed."

"He comes in the house? To your room?" Mason asked in a soft voice, then sent a worried glance to Serena.

"Only when Poppa's away."

"Do you love him, Anna?"

"Yes, I told you. Don't you believe me?"

"Of course, but I don't know anything about him. Tell me about him. What's his name?"

The sly look that crossed her face sent chills down Serena's spine. "Why? You gonna tell Poppa?"

"No, I wouldn't do that. I just want to help you."

"Why you keeping him from me?" Faith's brows drew together in anger, as Anna's voice lowered.

"Who?"

The door flung open sending Serena from her seat. Backing towards the bed, she whispered to Mason, "Wake her up."

"Anna, who do you think we're keeping from you?" Mason urged in a soft voice.

"Mason, wake her up," Serena whispered fiercely, feeling the air change around her. The door slammed shut.

"Dude." Ben's eyes were huge as he watched the meters in front of him.

Faith's sobs were a mixture of heartbreak and

anger. Serena glanced back to see Faith writhing on the bed clutching her stomach.

"Mason!" Serena hissed as the door sprung open once again.

"No! Poppa, No!" Anna's voice rose, echoing through the house.

"J'adoube!" Mason's voice was loud and clear as he spoke the word.

The door slammed shut and Faith bolted upright in the bed still screaming, "No!"

"Faith? Faith, are you ok?" Still standing in front of the bed, and Mason, Serena turned to her friend.

Faith blinked back the tears wrapping her arms around her stomach tightly.

"Breathe. You hear me? Breathe, dammit," Mason ordered firmly.

Faith sucked in a lungful of air then panted frantically. Serena found herself taking in a breath and letting it out slowly.

"Slow and easy, Faith. Calm down," speaking softer now, Mason tried to calm her.

After a moment, Faith found her voice. "What happened?"

"It's ok. It's over." Serena held out a bottle of water to her.

"I don't understand." Faith took the bottle then looked around the room slowly.

"Tell me what you are feeling right now," Mason gently coaxed.

"I'm sad. He's gone. Someone took him from me."

"Who? Who did they take?" Grabbing her arm, Mason pushed for the name.

"Jake." Faith pulled her arm from Mason's grasp.

"His name is Jake?" Sitting on the bed next to Faith, Serena gave Mason a fearful look.

"No, I don't think so, but I feel like it's Jake." Confused, Faith frowned at the unopened bottle of water in her hand.

"Do you smell anything?" Mason continued his questioning. His gold eyes intensely on Faith.

"Like what?" Faith blinked at him, her eyes still unfocused.

"Something burning?"

"No, I don't smell anything. I just want Jake. I need to see him." Tears started to gather in her eyes.

"Ok, hun." Serena patted Faith's knee. "I'll bring you home, if you want."

"No, call Jake. You can't keep him from me." The plastic protested as Faith's grip on the water bottle tightened.

"Faith, no one is trying to keep Jake from you." Concerned, Serena reached to grasp her shoulder. Mason stood, she could feel his frustration. Without saying a word, he left the room.

"I'll go call Jake, hun. You just lie here and rest." She patted Faith's shoulder and followed Mason shutting the door behind her.

Mason stood on the landing gripping the railing. His stance reminded her of how she had found him the day of the dress session.

"Mason, are you ok?" Serena asked covering his hand on the railing with her own.

"Yes. I'm fine." He grasped her hand in his.

"I wish you could tell me what's wrong."

"Ahh, love. Nothing..." Squeezing her hand, he looked away and sighed, "I just felt so close to getting the name from her, but honestly, I don't even know if that will help."

He smiled sadly at her. She pressed a palm to his cheek and gazed into his eyes. She hated the agony reflected in them. Not being able to help Faith wasn't the only thing bothering him. Serena could feel the heaviness weighing down his spirit.

Mason reached for her, pulling her to him. The kiss was soft and tender. Serena instantly felt the warmth growing inside her. Their magic was intact. He loved her still, but there was something he wasn't sharing with her. Wanting to take the pain from him, she kissed him back more urgently. He pulled back gently and sighed. "J'adoube."

"I don't understand, Mason."

"I adjust. It means I'm going to fix this, Rena. I have to." His words were desperate and his gaze filled with longing.

"Mace..." Before she could say anything else he swept her in his strong arms, dancing her a few steps to the doorway of his room. Their bodies moved as one, and she had to smile. Dancing with Mason, just as their lovemaking, was second nature. It seemed as though they had been doing it forever. Even with his muscular build, he moved gracefully and confident. He twirled her one last time and released her hand with a mischievous grin.

"You'd better see about your friend, love. We'll finish this later."

CHAPTER 21

Serena knew something had happened the day of the dress session. Mason still wasn't talking and Serena was still in the dark as to what it could be. He insisted it wasn't Richie, and the house had not warned her. Ben would have said if the meter went off, so she assumed it wasn't Richie. Mason's reaction to her in the dress had puzzled her. His declaration of being her husband, while odd, wasn't totally out of character. Since they met he had a habit of blurting out that statement as if someone was challenging their relationship. There were times when Serena was certain Mason wasn't even aware of uttering the words. Strangely enough, it comforted her. Their magic was real.

More information had come out at Faith's session, but Serena felt they were no closer to figuring it all out. Faith's obsession with Anna was growing, and her reality seemed to be mixing with the past. Serena wasn't comfortable with this development.

Serena watched Mason's chest rise and fall. He had finally fallen asleep on her daybed and she meant to let him sleep for as long as he needed. Moving quietly, she made her way from the daybed to sit at her desk. Something was keeping him up at night. No matter how many times he denied it, she knew better. The darkened circles under his eyes were all the proof she needed.

He still watched over her during the day, sought her out at night, and shared a bed. Their lovemaking was as passionate as ever, but she could still feel his distress. They had even finished their dance as he promised. He hadn't brought up the missing money, or the failed TV show since his return. Wondering if somehow that was the cause, she slipped silently out of the bookcase door to find Ben. Maybe he had picked up on something she hadn't. Hoping he would have more insight on the cause for Mason's sleeplessness, she closed the door with a soft click.

Walking through the parlor, her eye caught the candlestick on the mantle. Richie had been quiet. So had the house. Maybe Anna felt she had their attention now and didn't need to work so hard.

Serena noticed her reflection in the foyer mirror as she paused to listen to the house. The soft hum of the air-conditioning was the only sound she heard. Her own dark eyes stared back at her. She was still the same, but different in many ways. That young girl that had searched for so long had unintentionally found what she had been searching for. The magic of a home. Coeur du Bayou. Remembering the state of disrepair when she had first arrived, she felt proud of what she had accomplished here. With Mason's return and the wonderful friends she had found, she felt her life was full. The magic of belonging.

Her thoughts turned back to Mason and his strange turn of mood. She continued quietly up the stairs to find Ben. As she neared the landing, she could hear the click of a mouse and muttering coming from his room. Funny, she'd now probably consider it Ben's room even after he left. The thought of him leaving made her sad.

Knocking softly on the half open door, she called out, "Ben?"

"Yeah, come in."

"Hey, I wanted to talk to you." Serena pushed the door open to find Ben hunched over his desk in concentration.

"Ok. What's up?" Not bothering to glance at her, his focus remained on the screen in front of him.

"Did something happen at the dress fitting?"

"No, I told you. Nothing went off. EMF meter didn't even blink. I'm still going through the pictures, but I haven't found anything."

"Oh." Disappointed, she leaned against the doorjamb.

"Why?" Finally taking his eyes of the screen, Ben's curiosity got the better of him.

"Mason's been acting funny since that day. You saw him. Something happened."

"Yeah, that was weird, but Mason can be weird." Shrugging it off, Ben's gaze returned to the monitor.

"He hasn't said anything to you about it?"

"No."

"Don't you think he's been acting funny?"

"Hmm." Ben considered for a moment, then turned back to her. "I guess he has been kind of quiet now that you mention it."

"Right. No idea why?"

"No clue," he shrugged, then added, "Hey, while you're here. Take a look at this. I think I found Anna's grave back there in the cemetery. I've been digitally enhancing the pictures I took. This one could be hers."

Serena stepped closer to look over Ben's shoulder. The enlarged image of a headstone had pixels highlighted spelling out Anna's name. "Oh, wow. Ben, that's awesome! But that's not the big one."

"No, not the mausoleum. I'm going to try the library tomorrow. Do some research on the town. She mentioned them building it. Maybe somewhere in the records I'll come across information that would be helpful. Between the lumber yard and town officials maybe we'll get a better picture of the history of this place."

"Ben, you are a genius."

"Yeah, ok," he replied sarcastically.

"No really." She patted him on the shoulder, taking another look at the screen. "I wouldn't have thought to research the town's history."

"Hey, I don't feel stuff like you guys do, so I have to have other resources."

"So you think the town records will have something about the lumber yard and who owned it?"

"Or the mayor. This Harold guy's father. Maybe

the newspaper. See how far it goes back. Early 1900's. This place may have just been starting but there were other towns and bigger cities around by that time."

"I guess you're right. I never thought of what was here before... this." Serena motioned with her hands, flinging them out wide.

"Oh...wait a minute." Ben clicked frantically through the computer files.

"What?"

"Well, some of the audio...," he paused clicking through the files, "from before. It was really low and hard to make out. I didn't think it made any sense. Maybe it does, hang on."

"You didn't tell me about this."

"I know because I wasn't sure it was anything important. You know sometimes, you try to make something into what it's not, just because you want it so badly..."

Serena nodded. She knew that feeling exactly. She thought maybe that's what she had been doing with Mason when they first met. She wanted it to be magic so badly. When he had accused her so suddenly of planting the recorder, she had been doused with the reality that maybe it wasn't meant to be. So she had fled.

Ben looked up at her, his face serious. "I'm not going to make stuff up, Rena."

"I know Ben, but maybe you should have let us listen to it, too. Especially Mason, if it had something to do with what he experienced."

"Yeah, I guess, you're right. Things have been so crazy since I got here. Then Mason. I don't know. I just want to be sure. Here. Listen."

The sound of a door slamming came from the

speaker.

"*Faith?*" Mason's voice was unsure.

The thud of footsteps sounded, followed by a deep hoarse voice. "*No... ruin me... need support…..beat it out…….whore....*"

Some words were clear, others garbled. The ones that stood out to Serena were; 'ruin', 'beat' and 'whore'.

Looking into Ben's shocked face, she whispered to him, "Anna said something about a boat, didn't she?"

"Yes, she did."

He clicked a few more times and brought up the video of the last session. They both listened in silence waiting for her to bring up the boat.

Ben stopped the video when she did.

"Wow! That's a start. Hmm..." Ben looked at his watch. "I won't make the library today. Maybe I can try a few searches online and see what I come up with."

"Ok." Serena thought it over. "Do you think that's why the father didn't want them together because this Harold guy had connections?"

"Sounds like it." Ben nodded in agreement.

"I'll leave it to you then. Hungry? I can start supper." Serena smiled already knowing the answer.

"Always." He smiled at her. When she reached the door, he called out, "Rena?"

She turned, the serious, eager look had returned to his boyish face. "I'm going to figure this out. Don't worry."

"Now you sound like Mason." She gave him a small smile.

"He loves you, Rena. Nothing else should matter."

Shaking his head, he shrugged again. His simple logic stunned her. Nothing else should matter, but she wasn't that naive. Life had taught her that there was nothing simple about love or magic.

CHAPTER 22

Serena left Ben to do what he did best, research. Thoughtfully, she descended the stairs contemplating the voice on the audio. A shiver ran down her spine. It wasn't often she felt spooked, but knowing there were things going on around her she couldn't see was unnerving. The voice was angry. Even though the words were unclear, the intent was certain. She reached the foyer and caught her reflection in the mirror again. The faint scent of gardenia floated around her. She felt the house. Almost as if it sighed, at last content.

"Hey, anybody hungry?" Faith's voice came from the kitchen. Surprised, Serena headed their way to find out why Faith had returned unexpectedly.

"We brought food!" Faith held out two to-go containers as Serena entered the kitchen.

"Oh, I was just coming to fix us something. You guys didn't have to do that."

Jake came in the back door carrying three more food containers from the diner. "It's the special, but it was really good."

"We ate already, so there's plenty of extra." Faith smiled taking Jake's containers and setting them on the counter.

"Good, Reuben eats enough for two people." Serena laughed, then asked, "Where are the kids?"

"With David for a few weeks, before summer is over." Rolling her eyes, Faith automatically grabbed for napkins.

"What are y'all doing here?"

"Hey, I caught a spike." A wide eyed Ben came through the door. He glanced at Faith and Jake then zeroed in on the food. "Oh, hey…."

"They brought food for us."

"Alright." Grabbing a container from Serena's hands, Ben flipped the lid open. "Jackpot."

"Faith, why are you guys here?" Serena asked again.

"I want you to do a session with Jake."

At Jake's grumble, Serena asked, "But what does Jake want?"

"Look, I don't like this, but if it'll help, we can try it." Jake pulled at his shirt. "Does it have to be here?"

"No, we could go somewhere else. We could have come to your house." Ben looked up from the container.

"Yes, it has to be here!" Faith exclaimed. "Anna's here. She'll help you remember."

"It doesn't work that way and everyone is different. Some people aren't susceptible to hypnosis at all. It might not even work with Jake," Serena tried to explain. She didn't want Faith getting her hopes up.

"We have to try." Faith retrieved a fork from the utensil drawer and handed it to Ben.

"Let's eat and talk about this." Setting the container down, Serena motioned for them to sit, then lowered her voice. "Mason's asleep. I hate to wake him. He hasn't been sleeping much."

"I don't know how anyone can sleep in this house," Jake muttered, glancing longingly at the back door.

"Mason is awake, and I slept just fine." Rubbing his eyes, Mason strode in giving them all a wicked smile. "Is that food?"

"Did we wake you, hun?" Serena pushed the container towards him, noting the dark circles still under his eyes.

"No, I felt something. Is something burning?" Mason sniffed the air around him.

"No, but the EMF went off," Ben answered, taking his favorite seat at the kitchen island.

"It's because they're here together. I felt the house and smelled gardenias."

"Oh, you see? Anna's here!" Faith snorted, triumphantly.

"Wait. You smelled flowers. You smelled smoke." Using his fork, Ben pointed to Serena then Mason. "You both felt the house and my meter went off? All at the same time."

"What does that mean?" Jake backed hesitantly

towards the back door.

"I don't know, but something's going on." Ben shrugged diving into the food.

"They want us to do a session with Jake," Serena explained to Mason watching for his reaction.

"Ok." Nodding his dark head, he smiled at Faith.

"You guys go ahead and eat first." Faith grabbed another napkin for Mason, her ponytail dancing with her movement.

"I'll wait outside." Jake made his way to the door.

"I'll come with you." Faith hurried after Jake with a smile then turned back. "Just holler when y'all are done."

After the door shut, Serena found some forks and handed one to Mason.

"Are you sure you're up for this, hun?" Not knowing what was happening with Mason was enough of a concern to her, but she also knew how draining the sessions could be for him. She hated to add more stress.

"Yeah. I'm fine, love." Taking a seat next to Ben, he asked, "Did I miss anything else? It felt like I slept for a century."

"Our resident genius has located which grave is Anna's and thinks he may be able to track down some other information from what Anna has told us." Excited to share their good news, Serena hoped the information would lead to a breakthrough.

"I don't know if it'll help, but we can at least get a better picture of what was happening here at the time."

Mason nodded as he took a bite. "Mmm, this is good."

"There's extra if you need it." Serena smiled at

Ben's look of distress, then added, "There's another one for you, too."

"So, do you think Jake can handle this? That's the question," Mason asked as she took a seat next to him.

"I don't know. He doesn't seem too happy about this, so it may not even work." Since she first met Jake, she had noticed his agitation at being in this house. Serena began to doubt the logic of having the session at Coeur du Bayou at all.

"Next question is where?" As if reading her mind, Mason glanced in her direction. "Her room?"

"No, I don't think that's a good idea." Her dark curls bounced as she shook her head firmly.

"Well, he would have memories of that room according to what Anna told us," Mason argued.

"I'm just afraid that bringing him in that room might trigger something with the father. Mason, I don't want you to go through that again. And yes, before you ask, I am worried about you," Serena explained her reasoning.

"Ah, I see your point." Mason raised his eyebrows with a smile then asked, "Ok, in the parlor then?"

"Just use my room. I have everything already in there." Ben shrugged without looking away from the rapidly disappearing food in his container.

"Oh, ok." Surprised at the suggestion, Serena looked down at the unopened container in front of her.

"Done. Eat up, Rena."

⁂

"I don't understand why we can't use Anna's

room. It worked for me. She'll help. I know it." Faith paced by the door of Ben's room waiting for Jake to enter. When he didn't, she grabbed him by the hand and pulled him to the bed.

Moving out of the way, Serena sat in a corner chair behind Ben. Still not sure this was a good idea, she watched Faith nervously.

"Faith, you probably shouldn't even be here." Ben didn't bother looking up as he set a camera on the tripod near his equipment.

"I have to."

"No, you don't." Ben frowned at her over the monitor. "And it might not even work."

"Just stop." Jake took a breath and groaned it out. "I need to get this over with. Tell me what to do."

"Lie on the bed and relax." Mason entered bringing in a chair to set next to the bed.

"Yeah, right." Sitting on the bed, Jake kicked off his work boots in quick jerky movements.

"Try. Faith if you want to stay in the room, go sit over there and be quiet." With a flourish of his hand, Mason directed Faith towards Ben's corner.

"Maybe she should wait downstairs?" Unable to keep her doubts to herself, Serena asked from her perch behind Ben.

"But will she?" Ben asked sarcastically.

"No, I will not." Faith snorted and took a seat next to Serena, glaring in her direction.

"Fine. Ben when you have everything ready, let me know. Faith it's important you keep quiet. You are only here as an observer. Please remember that." Mason kept his voice low and even.

"Right." Faith sat up straight and nodded.

"I don't know how I'm supposed to relax when

everyone staring at me," Jake grumbled from the bed.

"Close your eyes. Take a few deep breaths. In through your nose, out through your mouth. Concentrate on your breath only. Fill your lungs, let it out slowly," Mason instructed.

The room started to settle as Jake's breathing grew more steady. Serena closed her eyes and let Mason's voice wash over her.

"Listen to my voice. Only my voice. When the session is over I will say the word reveille. When you hear me say the word reveille you will wake up refreshed with a clear memory of our discussion." Mason's rich voice filled the room with warm tones.

"Concentrate on the sound of my voice. I want you to think back to your earliest memory."

Jake let out a breath and sighed. "My mom rocking me."

"Before that... Before this life. Can you remember where you were?"

"It was dark. I think."

"Do you remember ever being in this house, Coeur du Bayou?"

After a sharp intake of breath, he began softly, "Ah, yes... I helped build this house. The finest house in town."

"You remember building the house?"

"Yes, we cut cypress from the bayou. The mill cut the planks so fine. I had never seen anything so fine." Jake's voice was filled with awe.

"Does the name Coeur du Bayou mean anything to you?"

"Yes, the bayou, it wraps around the property and meets up with the river in almost a heart shape, but there's another reason." His lopsided grin was a dead giveaway.

"A girl?"

"Yeah, there's a girl."

"Did you name the house for her?"

"No, it's not my house. It's her house. I made the sign. Her father paid me to make it. He wanted it in French."

"Why French?"

"So people would like him," Jake answered with such ease Serena began to relax.

"I don't understand. The people who live here? Don't you live here?"

"No, I don't live here. I come to work for him."

"Come from where?"

The room was still except for the gentle hum of the air conditioning as they waited for Jake to answer.

"Oh, yeah. The river." Jake turned his head as if recalling the direction. "We live across the river. I only come to work. I'm not like the people in town."

"How do you mean?"

"J'acadie. A Cajun."

"The girl is not?"

"No. She laughs when I speak French." At Jake's soft chuckle, Serena couldn't help but smile.

"What's your name?" Mason continued with the questions.

"Jacques."

Faith gasped loudly. Serena reached for her hand, squeezing it tightly.

"And the girl? What's her name?"

"I... I don't know. I can see her. When she laughs it makes me happy."

"Does she talk to you?"

"Yes, when her father's not around. Sometimes

she brings me food."

"What kind of food?"

"Pie." A giant grin spread across Jake's face. "She made a pie with the blackberries I picked for her."

"You bring her things?"

"I pick flowers. The gardenias are blooming. I leave them where she can find them. I painted some on the sign for her. It's our secret."

"You said you made the sign."

"Yes, her father paid me."

"Do you remember his name?"

"No, I don't think so. I know he didn't like me talking to his daughter."

"You loved her?"

"Yes, I did." His voice softened, then he gasped, "Anna. That was her name. I wanted to marry her."

"Did you marry her?"

After a short silence, Jake shook his head. "No, I don't think I did."

"Was there a baby?"

"A baby? No, I don't remember a baby."

"What do you re.." Mason's question was cut short by a snort from Faith.

"There was a baby," Faith blurted out.

"Shhh," Serena whispered squeezing her hand again.

"But there was a baby! Why doesn't he remember?"

"Dammit Faith," Ben growled through clenched teeth, glancing back to glare at her.

"I want you to wake up now, Jake. You will remember this session and the memories of your past life. Reveille," Mason instructed, his voice clear and calm.

Jake rubbed his eyes and yawned loudly. "Man, that wasn't too bad."

He gave Mason a lopsided grin then sat up slowly running a hand through his short brown hair.

"Jake, do you remember anything?"

"Oh yeah, I remember you asking questions and me answering. It was weird. Kind of like a dream. I was here, but it was foggy."

"Was I there?" Faith unable to contain her curiosity, spoke up.

"What?" Jake asked confused rubbing at his eyes again.

"Was I there? Do you remember me?" Faith sat forward pulling Serena's hand with her.

"It wasn't you, Faith." Jake shook his head. "It was Anna."

"I don't understand." Faith stared at him blankly.

"Faith you shouldn't have been here. He was just starting to remember," Mason said leaning forward to see Faith's face around Ben.

"Then why did you stop?" Faith snapped.

"Because you were getting upset," patting Faith's hand, Serena answered for Mason.

"Babe, what's wrong?" Jake swung his legs off the bed, his forehead wrinkled with concern.

"You don't remember me being there. How can you not remember me or the baby?" Faith stood shaking off Serena's hand.

"Whoa! Hey." Jake reached out a hand towards her, but she ignored it.

Faith ran from the room slamming the door behind her. Serena sent at awkward glance to Mason then Ben unsure of what to say.

Mason nodded to her then spoke up, "Jake, it

worked very well and I would suggest that we try again without Faith present. I think we can help you get rid of the anxious feelings you have here."

"Oh, ok." Jake nodded slowly reaching for his boots. "I do remember some of it, and the girl I remember isn't Faith. I know the difference."

"It's ok, hun." Serena smiled at him. "Why don't you go find Faith and bring her home?"

After the door closed behind him, Ben cleared his throat.

"What?" Mason asked, raking his hands over his face. Serena noted the circles under his eyes and worried that this session had taken too much out of him.

"Guys, this is weird. No readings at all." Ben held up the EMF meter and shrugged.

"Are you sure?" Serena asked bewildered. The room had been quiet and the only feelings she recalled were Faith's agitation.

"Nothing, not even a peep." Frowning, Ben put the gadget down rolling his eyes. "Which is weird that I find it weird now when it doesn't go off around here."

Mason considered for a moment letting the information sink in. "So Jake was actually remembering a past life, not having a paranormal encounter."

"Apparently so." Ben confirmed with a nod of his head but his voice was uncertain.

"Oh… So…" Serena turned wide eyed from Ben back to Mason.

"So Jake was actually Jacques and Anna is using Faith to see him again," Mason finished for her.

"Oh, dear."

CHAPTER 23

Last night she had the dream again. Parts of it had come rushing back to her throughout the day. Faith's laughter from the kitchen early that morning had sparked a memory of them all happily choosing dresses. Wedding dresses. Was that a premonition of their actual weddings or the new direction she was taking with Coeur du Bayou? After Richie had come for Claire last year, she thought the meaning of the dream was clear. More importantly, she thought it was over. Now she wasn't so sure.

Serena sighed over the yards of gauzy fabric she had ordered for the backdrops. Draping an end over the frame, she stood back to look at it. The white material reminded her of the dream. She didn't understand why she was still having it. Claire's cries from the dream haunted her. Claire was safe. Richie was gone. Well, almost gone.

Pulling the material back to the roll, she decided to move the frame in front of the window in the big room. The sunlight should come through for a lovely effect. If the wedding day came, and they were able to convince Evan to have it indoors, Serena wanted it to be spectacular. Luckily for her, the backdrop frames were portable. If Evan was still being hardheaded, she could move the whole production outside.

"Hey, where is everyone?" Ben's voice called from the foyer.

"In here. What's going on, Ben?" Serena met him at the entrance to the big room, hoping to keep him from waking Mason. He had finally drifted off on her daybed while she looked through wedding catalogs.

"I found something. The lumber mill was owned by one 'Leland Fox'. I'm pretty sure the names on the mausoleum are her parents."

"Ok, now we have names. Now what?"

"It's a start. I'm going to keep going through the records. Maybe something will jump out at me." Ben shrugged and glanced around. "Where's Mason?"

"Sleeping. I wish I knew what's keeping him up at night."

Before Ben could respond, the heavy front door opened and in breezed Eva Tremaine. Her short red hair framed her thin angular face and her pale blue eyes took in her surroundings greedily, as she dropped a heavy designer bag at her feet.

"Eva? What are you doing here?" Ben stepped in front of Serena, blocking her view.

"Reuben. Don't be rude. Take my bag up to my room. This place is magnificent. If you have the proof you put in your report, I'll have the camera crews here within the week." Not giving Ben time to argue, she started up the staircase. Her heels clacking hard on the wooden stairs.

"Serena… I didn't invite her here." Ben shook his head in disbelief as he turned to her.

"Where do you think you're going?" Serena stepped from behind Ben, her voice echoing up to the ceiling.

"Oh…" Eva paused in mid-step obviously surprised to see Serena there. "You're here too." Her pointy nose wrinkled in distaste. "Ben, is that wise? Having her here after the last mess she made."

"What?" Serena could feel the thundering of the blood pounding through her veins. "Get out!"

"No, I don't think so. I'm not going to let you ruin this for everyone a second time. Mason may have fell for you…" Eva paused slightly, then waved the thought away. "I don't care about that. The show is way more important."

"Get out of my house, now!" Serena's voice rose, and she felt the floorboards vibrate beneath her bare feet.

"Your house?" The stunned look returned to Eva's face, her ankle wobbled in her Jimmy Choo's and she grabbed the railing for support.

"Eva," Ben began in his calm voice, "I don't know how you found us, but I think you should leave. I'll carry your bag out for you."

"Yes, my house," Serena said firmly. "You need to leave."

A door slammed upstairs startling Eva.

"Where's Mason?" Her eyes wandered to the upstairs floor waiting for him to appear.

———— ✧✧✧ ————

Mason woke to a door slamming overhead. Bolting upright in Serena's daybed, he felt the air around him. Something was wrong. The faint smell of something burning had him on his feet. He felt anger and the raised voices from his dream came through the bookcase door. Springing the latch, he rushed through to the parlor.

"I thought you didn't care about Mason. I've asked you to leave. This is my house and I want you out," Serena's voice was filled with rage. Waves of red temporarily filled his vision.

"Rena, what's wrong?" He blinked away the redness.

"We have an unexpected visitor. I'm sure she's here to see you." Her dark eyes flashed dangerously to the staircase.

Following her gaze, he was shocked to find his ex-fiancé standing on the staircase glaring at Serena.

"Eva? What on earth are you doing here?" Mason blinked again.

"I came to help." Dusting off her white capris, Eva's voice was filled with purpose.

"I didn't ask her to come." Ben moved to pick up her bag.

"Help? Help with what?" Mason narrowed his eyes on Eva.

"The hauntings, what else? Ben's report is phenomenal. I can have a crew here by next week, ready to shoot." Her pale blue eyes gleamed with excitement.

Mason knew that calculated look. Somehow she had gotten a hold of Ben's report and figured she could just bully her way into calling the shots.

"No." His voice void of any emotion, Mason cursed the day he met the manipulative creature before him.

"What do you mean, no? What's going on here? You know what this could mean for us?" Her normal authoritative tone, had the slightest tinge of desperation.

"There is no us, and Serena has asked you to leave. Please leave." He motioned towards the door.

Eva's thin lips opened to argue as another door slammed upstairs. Mason watched as Eva pitched forward. Her face a mask of shock as she tumbled down the stairs sending a shoe flying.

"Eva, are you ok?" Ben dropped the bag and moved to help her up.

Mason reached her first, grabbing an arm.

"Who did that?" Red faced, she glared up the staircase as if looking for the culprit.

"What are you talking about?" Mason watched her curiously as he pulled her off of the floor.

"Someone pushed me," she spat.

"Are you hurt?" Ben grabbed her other arm gently.

"I'm fine." Pushing their hands away, Eva glared at Serena. "Just what are you up to here?"

"I don't know what you're implying." Serena folded her arms in front of her then continued, "All I know is this is my house. What happens here is none of your business."

"Someone pushed me. Who else is here? That

little shit, Sebastian?" Eva glanced around suspiciously, then hollered up the staircase. "Sebastian!"

"No, Sebastian is not here. I have no idea where he is, and no one else is in the house." Becoming impatient, Mason opened the door and held it.

"Eva, there's no one else here. If you're ok, I think you should go." Ben retrieved her shoe and handed it back to her.

"Yes," Mason agreed with Ben.

"This is not over. You're not moving ahead with the show without me." Unattractive blotches had formed on Eva's face as she hopped on one foot to put her shoe back on.

Ben picked up her case and ushered her out the door. Her grumbling and threats continued as the door closed behind them.

Mason could feel the anger still rolling off of Serena. Her dark eyes set on the closed door. "Are you alright, love?"

"Why is she here, Mason?"

"I don't know. Gabe told me she had been showing up at the office. Maybe she got the report that way." Mason tried to play it off, but the fact that Eva had ended up with information his brothers didn't even have wasn't sitting well with him.

"There's not going be a show." Her anger had calmed somewhat, but Serena's voice was firm.

"I know. Rena, I have no intention of ever doing that again." Damn Eva for showing up and stirring that pot. Mason had enough guilt to last him several lifetimes. The stupid TV show was of little consequence to him.

Ben came back through the door, a worried

frown on his face. "She's threatening to call the police."

"For what?" Mason turned on Ben. That blasted woman was determined to cause trouble for him.

"She says someone pushed her. There was no one there." Ben looked from Mason to Serena then back to Mason, "Right?"

"I didn't see anyone," Serena confirmed.

"I smelled something burning. The house woke me," Mason admitted worriedly, not liking where his thoughts were taking him.

"You think it was the house?" Ben's eyes were huge as he gazed back up the stairs.

Serena shook her head. "No, why would Anna do that? She doesn't know Eva. Eva has nothing to do with this. Richie maybe?"

"Wait. Richie wouldn't know her either." Ben shook his head.

"No, but Richie thinks I pushed him down the stairs the night he died. Maybe he pushed her." Using her hands, Serena explained her thinking.

"No." Mason felt the around him. "It wasn't Richie."

"Are you sure?" Hands now on her hips, Serena arched an eyebrow at him.

"Yes, it wasn't him. I didn't feel him," Mason struggled to explain, "There's a lot of sadness here, and some anger. Richie is different. There's a sense of danger and malice."

"Hold on. Are you saying the house pushed her?" Serena's face was uncertain as she thought it over.

"The house. Or Anna." Mason knew the burnt smell was attached to them somehow. The trouble was disconnecting one from the other.

"The house…" Ben rubbed a hand behind his head. "What if the house pushed Richie? Listen, the house protected you from Richie. The house warns you. You said it."

"I don't know." Now hugging herself, Serena looked to Mason for answers.

"The house warns you about Richie because he doesn't belong here," Mason reasoned with her. "Eva doesn't either."

"But how would it know?" Shaking her head again, Serena shrugged.

"I felt anger." Mason grabbed her shoulders softly and looked into her eyes. "But mostly from you. You didn't want her here."

"Are you saying it's my fault she fell down the stairs?" Serena stepped away from him and his accusation.

"No, I think the house knew you didn't want her here," Mason said simply.

CHAPTER 24

The wicked late summer heat had driven most people indoors. Noticing the empty streets, Serena wandered into the diner cautiously. Claire sounded upset on the phone, but refused to give any details. She had been adamant that Serena needed to come down to the diner to meet with her and Faith. Obviously in a lull between lunch and dinner, the tables were emptied and cleared.

"Claire, what's wrong?"

Turning in her stool to greet Serena, Claire gave her an apologetic smile. "Faith's upset. She doesn't understand why Jake didn't remember everything?"

Serena frowned as she took a seat next to her

friend. The owner and head cook, Gil, peeked through the order window and gave a little wave.

"She told you about that?" Serena lowered her voice.

"Yes, why? Was it another secret?" Claire pouted.

"Not from you. From Evan. We don't want to spook him anymore than he already is."

"Why doesn't Jake remember?" Claire whispered looking over her shoulder towards the kitchen.

"But he did remember." Serena knew the session with Jake had upset Faith, but she figured Jake had smoothed it over.

"That's not what Faith said." Claire shook her head confused.

"She wanted him to remember everything as vividly as she did. But it's different for everybody." Serena tried to phrase her words carefully. She didn't want to spook Claire either and she wasn't sure how to tell Faith about their suspicions about Anna.

"Oh, so it did work?" Claire sat up straighter on her stool.

"Of course it worked." Serena smiled at Claire hoping that would be the end of the conversation.

"Then why is she so upset?" Claire persisted.

"Hey. What's up?" Faith asked fishing her order pad out of her apron.

"Claire thought we could use a visit. I haven't really had a chance to talk to you since Jake's session."

Faith's eye narrowed on Claire. "You called her?"

"No." Claire's big blue eyes blinked rapidly, then closed. "Oh, ok. Yes, I did. I think maybe she can explain what happened."

"I was there," Faith snapped, pointing to herself. "I saw what happened. He didn't remember me."

"You?" Claire asked confused.

"Faith, he remembered a life before. It's not always clear. We're lucky it worked at all. He did remember Anna and gave us some details we didn't have before." Serena wasn't sure how else to make Faith understand.

"Really? Like what." Claire sat forward, elbows on the counter.

"His name." Intent on showing some kind of progress, Serena decided to add Ben's news. "And Ben has been doing some research. He also found Anna's grave."

"What?" Faith froze, the pad slipping from her fingers.

"Yes, it's back there in the graveyard. The mausoleum was for her parents."

"The baby? Is the baby there, too?" Faith's hands moved protectively over her stomach.

"No, nothing so far on the baby." Serena looked down at the counter, wishing Ben could be here to explain things.

"Then what good is that? I don't see how that will help any." Faith bent down to pick up the pad.

"We have names. That can lead to more info. If there is a baby there's bound to be a record of it somewhere," Serena explained patiently, looking to Claire for help.

"There was a baby. I don't know why he didn't remember, but there was a baby," Faith's voice rose in desperation as she stood back up.

"Faith, you ok?" Gil called from the kitchen.

"Yeah, I'm fine. Just girl stuff." Faith smiled at

him as he popped his shaggy blonde head through the order window.

"Hmmm, yeah, ok." Gill rolled his eyes at Faith then groaned loudly as something caught his eye outside. "Oh, no. Not again. Tell her we're closed."

They followed his gaze through the plate glass window to see Eva getting out of a dark SUV. She turned back to speak to the driver for a moment, then slammed the door shut.

"Maybe she won't come in," Faith said hopefully then groaned as Eva reached her car then turned back towards the diner, obviously deciding whether or not to go in.

"I thought she left," Serena muttered miserably.

"You know her?" Faith whispered.

"Oh yeah, unfortunately. She's Mason's ex."

"She's a cunt. That's what she is," Gil declared loudly.

"Gil!" Claire exclaimed with a giggle then covered her mouth with her hand.

"She complained about my meatball stew. That's one of my best selling plates." Ready to defend his prowess in the kitchen, Gil brandished a spatula and shook it at the window.

Serena laughed at Gil's performance, then turned back towards the window. Eva took another step towards the door then stopped when she noticed Serena watching her. Not wanting to drag her friends into the drama, Serena headed out the door to meet her.

"What are you still doing here?" Not bothering with a greeting, Serena got right to the point.

"Aren't you going to invite me in for coffee?" Eva smirked at the window.

"Sorry, they're closed." Hand on hip, Serena nodded to her friends through the diner window then turned back to the redhead whose pale skin was already turning a sickly shade of pink. "The only reason I can imagine you're still hanging around is my house. You're not welcome there. I don't think I can make it any more clear."

Pursing out her lips, Eva thought a moment. "Really? Well, I think you've left out a few details that the others may find interesting. This time Mason will have to believe me."

"What do you mean 'this time'?"

"You'll see. Mason is blind where you are concerned. He'll soon see you for what you are." She pointed a red tipped nail in Serena's face.

Taking a step closer to Eva, Serena demanded, "What am I?"

"Ladies…" Evan's voice followed by his footsteps on the pavement broke the tension. "Serena, what's going on?"

Eva backed away from Serena quickly, smiling at Evan. "Just catching up, Officer." With one last smirk in Serena's direction, Eva climbed in her car and drove away.

"Something tells me she's not a friend." Evan watched the taillights of the sporty white Cadillac until it turned off the main street.

"She's not. She's just trying to make trouble."

"What kind of trouble?" Evan frowned down the empty street.

"Evan, it doesn't concern you." Serena started to turn away. The last thing she needed was Evan asking questions.

"Wait a minute." Evan grabbed her arm. "Who is

she?"

"Mason's ex." She shrugged.

"Really?" He dropped his hand and looked back down the street.

"What? Not impressed?" Laughing at his expression, she felt a little lighter.

"No, not impressed. Actually a little disappointed in Mason. She's kind of a…" Evan tilted his head as if trying to formulate an appropriate word.

"Cunt?" She supplied for him.

He coughed in surprise. "Hey now. I was going to use a different word, but yeah."

"Gil's word, but it fits."

Evan chuckled, "Well, now I know who's been teaching my sister that foul language. I'll have to talk to him. You ok?"

"I'm fine."

"Should I be worried?" Evan was studying her closely.

"About?"

"About what you and the other two in there are up to?" He jerked a thumb in the direction of Claire and Faith watching them through the window. "And now I'm not so sure about Gil."

"Just wedding plans, I promise." Holding up her hands, she smiled sweetly at him. "So you're here to meet Claire?"

"I saw the cars so I thought I'd stop. Then I saw you about to do something stupid, so I figured I'd interrupt."

Serena frowned up into his stern face. "I wasn't going to do anything stupid."

"I've seen that look before. You were about to blow." He folded his arms over his chest knowingly.

"Wait, did you see who dropped her off? Was it someone from here?" Serena wiped at the sweat forming on her brow.

"I didn't recognize either vehicle."

"Where would she stay?" Serena asked as she stared down main street.

"Are you asking me?"

"No, I mean… there's nowhere to stay in town. She had to stay somewhere." Serena narrowed her eyes as she thought it over.

"The nearest hotel is about twenty miles. Am I gonna have to tell you not to leave town?"

"Hmmm…" She turned back to see Evan watching her suspiciously. "Oh, no, brother dear." Using Faith's term of endearment, she took his arm then added, "But don't search my car. You might find a shovel or bolt cutters."

Evan chuckled as they walked to the door of the diner together. When she stopped outside the door, he asked, "Aren't you coming in?"

"No, tell Faith and Claire I'll talk to them later."

Driving back through town, Serena kept an eye out for the SUV and Eva's Cadillac. Cypress Point wasn't very big, so her search didn't last long. Aside from her house and her interest in Mason, Serena couldn't imagine why Eva was still in town. Eva's threats didn't mean much to Serena. She hadn't been the one to sabotage the investigation or steal the money, but obviously someone wanted Mason to believe she had. Eva's little slip up had Serena betting it was her. What better way to get back at her and

Mason for ending their engagement?

Pulling into the long drive way of Coeur du Bayou, the house demanded her attention. She was drawn to it. This was her home. She had lovingly and painstakingly restored it from shambles to its stately nature. She belonged here.

Looking again, she could see what Eva saw. The TV crews would have a field day with the abundance of scenic shots. To Eva it was nothing more than a set, and a means to an end. To her fame seeking eyes, it was a gold mine. To Serena, it was home. Her sanctuary away from the funny looks and snide remarks.

She understood Ben's search for proof and the appeal it would have to most people. But she knew things. She felt it. It was her magic. It didn't matter what other people thought or believed. She knew what she knew. Nothing would change that. Eva could plot and plan, but nothing would change her mind. Pausing at the door, she touched it softly resolving that Coeur du Bayou's story, ghosts, and secrets would remain private. The house welcomed her as she opened the door, enveloping her in a warm golden light.

"There you are," Mason's worried voice sounded from the parlor.

"Sorry, hun. You were sleeping. I hated to wake you just tell you I was going to meet Claire and Faith at the diner."

"Oh, everything alright?" Mason came to her, wrapping her in loving hug. She melted into him and sighed. Pulling away he looked into her face. "What's wrong?"

"I saw Eva in town. Why is she still here?"

"Eva?"

"Yeah, she got out of a dark SUV while I was at the diner. Would she know anyone in town?"

"Not that I know of. She's probably just trying to find out about the house."

"It's my house," Serena mumbled to herself.

"I know. Rena, look at me." Waiting until she looked up at him, Mason locked eyes with her. "You have to know she can't come between us."

"No, but she'll try, Mason. She practically threatened me." The heat had taken most of the fight out of her. She felt as wilted as her sundress that stuck to her sweaty body.

"What?" Mason's jaw clenched in anger.

"She said you'd have to believe her 'this time'." Serena pulled at the damp material clinging to her legs.

"This time?"

"Meaning you didn't believe her before. Was it her that made you think I sabotaged the investigation?" Serena watched his reaction carefully. She knew Eva was unaccustomed to not getting what she wanted.

"No…" Mason ran a hand through his hair as he paced. "She wasn't there. And why would she take the money?"

"Hey…" Ben walked into the room stopping in mid-sentence awkwardly. "Whoa… What's going on?"

"Was Eva there?" Mason turned to him, his green gold eyes honing in on Ben.

"Where?"

"At the shoot for the investigation. You said you had video of everyone that went through that room.

Was she there?"

"I don't remember seeing her, but I can go back through. Why?" Ben seemed reluctant to hash it over all again.

"She just threatened Serena. Something about me having to believe her 'this time'." Mason's eyes narrowed on Ben. "And how did she end up with your report?"

"I don't know. I didn't send it to her." Ben turned away from Mason's accusing stare to Serena, hoping for her support.

Mason stared at him for a moment then shook his head.

"No, but Gabe did say she had been showing up at the office. Maybe she took it while that girl I hired wasn't looking. I need to call Gabe to see if she's been there recently."

"Ok."

At Ben's less than enthusiastic response, Mason asked, "What Ben?"

"I don't understand. She wanted it more than anyone. Why would she do that? And what can she do about it now? It doesn't make any sense." Shoving his hands in his pockets, he shrugged.

"To get me out of the way," Serena answered him. "She practically said that."

"There's no way she can come between us," Mason said again. Serena felt his heat from across the room.

"Well, last time it worked for three years." Serena shook her head sadly. "And not to hurt your feelings, but that show still means more to her than any of you."

CHAPTER 25

"You look terrible." Faith looked over her shoulder at Serena as she entered the kitchen. The scene had become all too familiar. Faith cooking. Ben eating. Their normal routine. They had formed an odd sort of family and Serena was thankful.

Ben nodded in agreement from his favorite spot. "I thought it was Mace that was having trouble sleeping."

"Yeah, I keep having that dream, and Mason wasn't here. I've gotten used to having him around." Serena didn't mind admitting how quickly she had grown accustomed to having him close. Waking from the dream in a frantic state and finding herself alone had been more distressing than the dream itself.

"With the dresses? Still?" Ben's curious gaze made her pause.

"That's weird." Faith flipped a pancake unto the cast iron griddle. "Do you think it's Richie?"

"I don't know…" Rubbing at her temples, Serena tried to shake the uneasy feeling left by the dream.

"Is it the same dream, or has it changed?" Ben tapped his fork anxiously on the empty plate in front of him.

"No, it's the same dream. We're here in the house picking out dresses. Everything gets dark. There's blood on the dress. Then I can hear Claire crying, but I can't find her."

"Hmm." The tapping stopped as Ben considered.

"What?" Pouring coffee into a mug, Serena inhaled the delicious aroma.

"I don't know. I'm not much on dreams but I don't know why you'd still be having it unless something else is going to happen." The tapping started again.

"Why did Mason leave?" Faith asked, a frown formed on her face.

"He had business to take care of. I think he had to meet with his brother." Serena stifled a yawn.

"When's he coming back?"

"I'm not sure. I figure he'd be back in a day or two. Is something wrong?" Warming her hands on the mug, Serena held it close to her heart.

"I just wanted to talk to him about Jake. Why didn't he remember?"

"Faith, he did remember. We talked about this." Sighing, Serena put her cup down on the counter. Obviously their talk at the diner hadn't done any good.

"No, it was different. He didn't remember me." Faith turned her back to Serena.

"But it wasn't you. He remembered Anna."

"No. Like I remember the guy, but it felt like Jake." Waving the spatula with one hand, Faith arched a brow at her to get her point across.

Ben and Serena exchanged uneasy glances.

"Faith." Serena rubbed at her temples again, sighing. "He remembered a past life. I told you it's not always clear. Most people don't remember anything at all."

"But it was me, right?" Taking the last pancake from the griddle, Faith carefully placed it on a stack.

"No, Faith. It wasn't you." Putting his fork down, Ben watched the stack intently as Faith picked up the plate.

"Ben, don't," Serena warned.

"Rena, she doesn't understand," Ben answered her, then turned to Faith in a calmer tone. "Faith, listen to me. Anna is here. You've seen her, right?"

"Yes, I did." Faith nodded hesitantly, placing the stack of pancakes on the island counter within Ben's reach.

"She shows you her memories?" Ben locked eyes with Faith even as he slid the plate closer to his.

"Yes," Faith agreed with more enthusiasm.

"You can't be her if she's already here." Ben shrugged, lifting his hands at the revelation.

Serena bit her lip and waited for Faith to connect the dots.

"What?" Faith's eyes narrowed on Ben, her pony tail shaking vigorously. "No, that can't be right."

"Yes, think about it." Picking up his fork again,

Ben pointed it at Faith. "She attached herself to you because of Jake."

"No, I felt it." Hand clutching her apron, Faith looked around the room breathing heavily. "You found her grave?"

"Yeah."

"I'm going out there." Pulling the apron overhead, she left it on the counter. "I remember. I was her."

Not waiting for a response Faith stalked out, slamming the door behind her, letting in a draft of warm air.

"I'm sorry, Rena."

"I don't know if that was a good idea."

"She was getting too emotional. That's not going to help anyone." Using his fork, Ben picked up half the stack and transferred it to his plate.

"You're right. I've been growing more concerned about her. She's so distressed that Jake didn't remember her or the baby." Serena watched as Ben began to pour syrup over the pancakes. The sweet smell reached her nostrils, turning her stomach.

"I didn't want to say anything in front of her, but about your dream..." Ben looked up from the river of syrup that now pooled around the stack encasing it in a sticky shell.

"My dream?" Confused at his turn of topic, she glanced down at her untouched cup of coffee.

"Yeah, you say you were trying to find Claire, but you never say what happened to Faith. Where was she when it got dark?" Ben snapped the lid of the syrup closed and waited for her reply.

"I don't know."

—————— ⚬⚬⚬ ——————

Mason stood at the bar of his parents' greatroom, his hands dropping ice cubes into the tumbler before him. The clinking sounded unfamiliar to his ears. He had dreamed of Serena, of course. The cursed memory would never leave him. His main discomfort on this day was not regret, but anger. The detective had left quickly after giving him the disturbing news.

Serena had not been found because she had not been using her name, which he already knew. What he hadn't known was that Serena had been working for his main competition in the paranormal investigation business, Sentinel.

Sentinel's owner, Graham Young, had used the capital and resources generated by his alarm business to start up his own ghost hunting team. He personally had done his best to upstage Mason's investigations. Going behind them and capturing video of questionable apparitions after Spirit Catchers hadn't found anything. The devious bastard must have recruited Serena as soon as she left him.

On the upside, there was no evidence that she had taken the money. He had secretly hoped for that all along, but his suspicious nature kept him doubting.

"Who was that?" His brother's deep voice startled him causing the whiskey to splash haphazardly against the glass.

"Private Investigator," Mason said without turning to look at his brother.

"Oh, ha. I hope you got your money back," Gabe chuckled.

"What?"

"If he was supposed to find Serena for you, I think he failed miserably." Pointing to the drink in Mason's hand, "Kind of early, even for you, isn't it?"

"I don't know why I poured this." Mason sniffed at the tumbler, then put it back on the bar.

"What's going on Mace?" Gabe took a seat, obviously concerned with his brother's behavior.

"Eva showed up at Serena's."

"Because? Ah, don't tell me. She's still madly in love with you. Good god." Gabriel's exaggerated eye roll was meant to lighten the mood, but Mason was numb with anger.

"No, that would be Sebastian's story. Apparently she's bound and determined to get that TV show."

"And she needs you? How did she even find you?" Leaning back into the arm chair, Gabe waited for the story.

"She got a hold of Ben's report. I'd like to know how. If that girl I hired gave it to her, she's fired." Mason paced in front of the bar, running his hands through his hair.

"Report? What kind of report?"

"Here. I wasn't going to mention it, but even you might find it interesting." Mason picked up the file and handed it to his brother.

Skimming through the papers briefly, Gabe seemed uninterested until he came across the photo of Claire at the top of the stairs.

"Pretty girl. Hmm. What's this shadow? Photoshopped?"

"No, Ben took that picture."

"Reuben? You two have been working an investigation this whole time?" Closing the folder, he slapped it on his knee.

"It's Serena's house. She called Ben for help. That's how I found her."

Gabriel's laughter echoed through the room. "I certainly hope you got your money back. Serena found a haunted house, imagine that."

"Eva saw the report and came running. TV crew just waiting for her signal."

"What's the problem?" Gabe frowned at him.

"Serena doesn't want anything to do with it. It's her home. Some of her friends have had experiences there that are personal. She doesn't want them exploited."

"Fair enough. Again, what's the problem?"

"Eva threatened Serena. She said 'this time' I'd have to believe her." Mason watched as Gabe sat up straight in his chair. When his brother didn't comment he continued, "Not even an hour later, I get a phone call from the P.I. needing to meet with me because he has new information."

Gabriel narrowed his eyes on Mason, then howled with laughter. Strands of salt and pepper hair fell loosely around his face as his body shook with amusement.

"What is so funny?"

"Please tell me he thinks he found Serena after all this time," Gabe chuckled, wiping at his eyes.

Grimacing at his brother's obvious enjoyment he answered truthfully, "No, last time I was here I met with him. I told him I found Serena and put him on something else."

"What? Have you lost your mind? You gave him more money?" Gabe's blue eyes rounded incredulously as his voice lost all traces of mirth.

"I need to know who set us up and stole the

money."

"Money?"

"I had some cash on hand at the office. It went missing right after everything fell apart."

"Mason, someone stole money and I'm just hearing about this now?" Gabe stood impatiently. "Did you report it to the police?"

"No, it had to be one of us. The safe, the security code, the key to the office."

"Oh, for the love of Christ!" His brother's voice echoed through the cavernous room.

"Gabriel!" Noemi's voice stopped them both.

"Mom. Sorry, I am just stunned at the stupidity of your son."

Mason turned to greet Noemi. Before he could speak she demanded, "What money?"

"I'm just hearing about this, too," Gabe grumbled sitting back down.

"I put money, cash money, in the safe at Spirit Catchers in case something unexpected came up. It was my money. I was just trying to cover any expenses." Mason began to pace again; he knew it sounded rehearsed. He had gone over it a thousand times in his head.

"When?"

"After the botched attempt at the TV pilot."

"Did Serena have the code?" Gabe asked the most logical question.

"No, not that I know of."

"She didn't take the money." His mother's green eyes glinted with disapproval.

"No, she didn't. She says she didn't and I believe her." Frustrated, Mason dropped his shoulders. He wanted desperately to believe her, but the anger

MAGIC

simmered and nagged at him.

"So that leaves who? Me? Ben? Sebastian?" Exasperated, Gabe sat on the edge of his seat.

"And Eva," Mason reminded him.

"Oh, I see. She got her hands on Ben's files so you're thinking she has a way into the office."

"Yes."

"What exactly did the investigator have that was so upsetting it has you pouring whiskey this early?" Gabe motioned to the untouched tumbler on the bar.

"I can't talk about it." Mason turned away to pace again.

"Yes you can." Standing, Gabriel waved the folder in front of him. "I will not be the last to know everything going on around here. Tell me."

"Serena has been working for Sentinel for the last three years."

"Starting when? Before or after she left?"

"After, from the information he gathered. Bank transactions, phone records and he even snapped a picture of her meeting with Graham. Not only has she been helping with their investigations, he's been recommending her to people for private readings and what not."

"Mason, I know you're upset and taking this personally, but she had to take care of herself," Noemi's voice softened with reason.

"Why him? Of all people, why him?" Mason knew his anger was unreasonable, but the memory that haunted him had taken on a new element. Thanks to the P.I., the man in the shadows now had a face. Real or not, his mind grabbed a hold of the image and wouldn't let it go.

"Mom's right, you can't fault her for supporting

herself. And surely you're not thinking they were romantically involved?"

"Three years. If it wasn't him, there had to be someone." Mason's gaze wandered back to the whiskey.

"Get ahold of yourself. You're not thinking straight." Walking over to the bar, Gabe grabbed the tumbler and dumped it in the sink.

Mason knew the images would continue to torture him until he talked to Serena in person. She wouldn't lie to him directly. He would know.

"I'm going back. I have to talk to her."

Ben's question haunted her throughout the day. Serena had focused on Claire because of her cries. Feeling compelled to find her, she had walked through the darkened rooms searching. Faith had vanished also, but not as dramatic. She had just faded into the darkness. Was that significant? She wasn't sure. Sitting at her desk, Serena felt just as lost and confused as she had that morning. The only thing she was absolutely sure of was that she belonged here in this house.

"Hey Rena." Ben tapped lightly on the open bookcase. "I'm getting ready to leave."

"Hmm."

"I told you about that shoot. Wedding shoot. Michelle referred me."

"Oh, wow, yes. I'm really happy things are working out."

"Yeah, it's good to have connections."

"Will she be there?"

"I don't know why she would. She just sold the dress." Ben rolled his eyes at her.

Serena hid a smile as she followed him out. Ben retrieved his bags from the foyer then turned to frown at her.

"Just wondering. I didn't know how close y'all were." Shrugging, Serena pushed the curls from her neck.

"Close?" Ben groaned opening the door. "Just stop right there."

"Fine. Just tell her I said hi."

"I told you, she won't be there." Ben headed out the door with one last frown.

"Yeah, ok."

"Are you sure you'll be alright?" Stepping off the porch, he turned back to look at her.

"Yes. Ben, I'm fine."

"Mason didn't answer when I called to let him know I was leaving. I'm sure he's probably on his way back by now."

"Yeah, I'll be fine," Serena said absently as her gaze caught Faith's light blue sedan still in the driveway. "Faith's still here."

"I guess."

"She never came back in." Serena stepped off the porch to peer in the direction of the wooded path.

"I haven't seen her since she said she was going to the graveyard this morning."

A feeling of dread came over Serena. "That's been hours."

"What's wrong?"

"I don't know. It's too hot out here. She wouldn't still be out there."

"Come on. Let's go find her." After placing his

bags in his Land Rover, he slammed the door and took off down the path.

The summer heat was stifling on its own but mixed with heady woodsy scents, Serena found it difficult to breath. Within minutes her light summer shirt was clinging to her.

"Are you sure she wasn't in the kitchen?" Ben asked wiping at his brow.

"No, I would have heard her. I thought she had left."

As they neared the small cemetery, the sound of sobbing reached them.

"Faith?" Serena called out as she picked up her pace.

Upon entering the clearing, they found Faith sitting on the ground her back against a headstone, head in her hands, sobbing uncontrollably. Serena knelt beside her.

"Faith, are you alright, hun?"

Strands of hair, slick with sweat, stuck to her face and neck. With red puffy eyes, Faith looked up at Serena. "He's gone."

"Who?"

"Jacques. My father came home. Jacques told him about the baby and that we were getting married."

"Faith, calm down." Ben leaned over to rub her back gently. Faith's hiccoughing sobs became more frequent as she became more distressed. "Just breath for a minute."

"No, no, no." Her sobs continued.

"She needs water, and shade." Motioning with his head to the tree line, Ben pulled Faith off of the ground. "Let's get her to the shade and I'll run back to the house for water."

"He killed him." Faith grabbed at Ben's shirt. "Why? Why would he do that?"

"Killed who?"

"I saw. My father killed Jacques. He beat him with his hands."

"Calm down." Sitting her under a tree, Ben looked at Serena. "Try to get her to calm down."

"Jake. I need Jake, please." Faith hugged her knees.

"Ok, I'll be right back." Ben hurried off down the path.

"It's alright, hun." Serena sat next to her. "Tell me what happened."

"He killed him. He said I wasn't going to ruin his plans for the gambling boat. He was so angry like he was possessed or something. He kept beating him. There was blood everywhere. I thought he was going to beat me, too. He said he needed me to marry Harold." Faith pushed at the sweaty strands of hair miserably. Her ponytail had fell to one side, hanging limply as she gave in to another sob. "I told him I wouldn't marry him, I loved Jacques. He hit me. I ran to my room. He followed me up the stairs. He said I'd never see Jacques again. Never again. Never again."

CHAPTER 26

Serena sighed, unlocking the heavy wooden door to Coeur du Bayou. She was glad to be home, even if she was alone. Funny how things changed. She had gone from always being alone to always having someone else around. Mason had not yet returned. Ben had finally left for his shoot after helping her get Faith and her car home safely. She put her keys on the entryway table and glanced at her reflection in the mirror. The humid heat had her hair a wild mess. Her curls had escaped their tie and clung to her back. Feeling the stickiness from her earlier outdoor ordeal with Faith, she paused deciding if she needed a shower or tea first. The shower won out and she headed up the stairs.

A noise from the parlor stopped her cold. She knew she was alone. Walking softly down the stairs, she tiptoed into the parlor listening for more noises. Not sensing any movement, she made her way in the darkness to the closest lamp. Serena held her breath as she felt for the switch. The soft light warmed the room and the bright jewel tones put her instantly at ease. Releasing the breath, she glanced around for the source of the noise. Everything seemed to be as she had left it. Her gaze continued around the room finally landing on the fireplace mantle. One lone candlestick stood directly in the middle of the mantle. Not where she left it. Richie. Feeling the room around her, she wondered why the house hadn't warned her. Then again, she had been preoccupied today with her worries about Faith.

"Not tonight, Richie," Serena muttered to the empty room. Crossing to the mantle, she placed the candle stick back where it belonged. Something still felt off, but she couldn't place it. To be on the safe side she lit some incense and made her way back upstairs. If Richie was going to act up tonight, he could wait until after her shower.

Still unsettled, Mason drove through the darkened town of Cypress Point. He thought the long drive would give him time to calm down. Why hadn't she mentioned working for Graham, if it was only work?

Because he'd be upset and jealous. He knew the answer. He couldn't fault her for that, but surely since they were trying to work things out she'd tell him the truth. Did Ben know? His suspicious nature had him wondering if Ben had kept her secrets.

What did that matter? he chastised himself. She had called Ben. Not him. Mason supposed he was still upset about that. Serena was here now, with him. Stop being so foolish. You trust them both. His mind ran back to the sabotage and the missing money. If they were in it together, Ben could have helped her pull it off or at the very least looked the other way.

No, Ben wouldn't do that. Running a hand over his face roughly as he pulled up to the house, he noticed that only Serena's car was in the driveway. She was here. Alone. The interior light flooded the inside of his car as he searched for his phone. Sometime during the drive it must have fallen to the floorboard. Reaching over to fish a hand around the passenger side leg well, he felt an envelope. Curious, he pulled it and felt the weight of his phone pinning it down. Looking at his phone first, he noticed the notification light flashing. Two missed calls from Ben and a text.

Hey man. Wanted to remind you I have a shoot. Leaving now.

"Ok, see? You're being paranoid for nothing. Go in and talk to her." Reasoning with himself, he opened the unfamiliar envelope to find a photograph. Pulling it from the manila envelope, his eyes focused on the subject and his vision immediately went red. On the enlarged photo was a smiling Serena walking arm in arm with Evan, her dark curls flowing behind her. She had on the same dress she'd worn the day before. A note attached read: *She's not what you think.*

No. Even as he tried to talk his mind out of what

he was seeing he thought back to the night he arrived at Coeur du Bayou. The deputy had seemed more than a little over protective of Serena. His first assumption had been that there was something between them.

The memories danced before him. Her. It was always her, but now the man in the shadows had a different face. The dark headed deputy held her, caressing her as she moved to the music. The face periodically interchanging with Graham Young's.

A shadow moved in front of the window of the house. The anger built with each thundering beat of his heart.

Feeling better after her shower, Serena took her tea into the parlor still pondering why the house had not warned her. She lit another incense, watching the flame grow. Something still felt off. Blowing out the flame, she glanced at the mantle again. The candlestick was sitting innocently in its place exactly where she had left it.

She felt him suddenly. A surge of longing pulsed through her. Mason. Making her way to the window, she was relieved. She moved the curtain aside to peer outside. Yes, he was home. He appeared to be just sitting in his car watching the house. Not opening the car door, until he noticed her in the window. Something was wrong, she could tell by his movements. Wanting to help, she went to the door to greet him.

The door swung open before she reached it. Mason was there suddenly in front of her, his eyes glowing with anger. His breath ragged and raspy, "Why?"

"Mason, what's wrong?"

"Why didn't you tell me? How long has it been going on?"

He shoved a picture in her face.

"What? How long what?"

"You and the deputy?" he snarled at her.

"No. Oh no. There is nothing going on." Snatching the picture from his hand, she glanced at the familiar scene. "Did Eva give you this? She must have gotten someone else to take this. She had just drove away. I watched her leave. That bitch had someone watching me."

"Has he been here?" Mason looked around the room wildly.

"What?" Serena blinked at the accusation. He still didn't trust her.

"Has he been here today? While I was gone?"

"No, Mason. You need to calm down." She tried to reach for him, wanting to sooth the anger.

"What else haven't you told me?" Mason grabbed her arms forcing her to look at him. The heat between them grew. Serena looked into his eyes and remembered. His anger. Like this but another time.

The memory flickered before her. Blood on the lace dress, Mason's face as he stood over her. There was pain. She heard her own voice pleading with him to stop.

"Stop, Mason." Unsure of what she was seeing or feeling, Serena shook her head.

"Why are you lying to me?" His hands gripped her harder, digging into her flesh.

"Let me go!" She pushed at him, backing slowly

to the stairs.

He followed, his rage exploding from him. "You whore!"

"No, Mason," she whispered as the air around them became thick and heavy. A crashing sound came from the parlor. The candlestick. Richie. The memory flashed again before her. Blood and pain. The controllable anger vibrating from the man she loved.

"Where's my money?" The strange voice that came from Mason echoed through the house.

"Mason, stop. I don't have your money," she hissed at him. "I didn't lie."

"You've been seeing Graham. I know."

A gasp escaped her lips. "No."

"Lying whore."

"It wasn't like that. It was a job." The first flicker of fear ran through her. His anger filled the room. His eyes and stony expression brought the memory back. Mason as he was then, screaming obscenities, his weight pressing down on her. Her voice pleading desperately as she felt the knife pierce her stomach. The pain blinded her as he slashed again and again.

"You!" Stunned at the horrible memory, time felt frozen as she lifted a finger to point at him. Then fear took over sending her running up the stairs. Mason let loose a dangerous growl, and followed. Serena felt his muscular arms wrapping around her legs. She fell helpless as his weight dragged her down hitting the stairs hard. Her ribcage taking the brunt of the fall. Gasping for breath, she was trapped under him as he climbed up her body. The wooden edge of the stair pushing harder into her side. He turned her over finally, and she swung at him. Her fist connecting with the side of his face.

"You... You did it. You killed me." Every breathless sob sent shooting pains throughout her body.

Mason's expression changed from cold to horrified. His hands loosened on her and he moaned, "Oh, Rena... No."

"Get away from me!"

"No, Rena, please. I didn't mean to hurt you."

"Get off!" She pushed herself up the stairs backwards, kicking her legs loose and untangling herself.

"Rena, I'm sorry."

"Take your pictures and accusations and get out of my house!" Her voice was fierce.

"No, I won't leave you alone. Something's not right." Mason shook his head gazing into the air around him.

"Yeah, I'm getting that, but it's you." Moving slowly, she watched him warily and used the railing to pull herself up. The lights flickered and hummed. The aroma of wet dog floated around her.

"No, not now," she whispered.

"Rena, please," still on his knees, Mason pleaded with her. "He's here. He wants to hurt you."

The lights flickered again, wildly this time. The odd hum grew louder.

"You should just leave. Go away, Mason." The lights went out before she finished speaking, his name falling into darkness.

Scrambling the rest of the way up the stairs, she crouched against the railing.

"Rena!" The howl that came from Mason shook the house.

Staying low, she felt with her hands along the

floor to find the nearest wall. She groped along it, making her way safely away from the staircase. If she stayed up here, she knew she was trapped.

Trapped. The vision of Mason leaning over her with bloody hands brought tears to her eyes. What kind of magic had brought them together? *"Careful what you wish for, girl."* Her grandmother's constant warning echoed in her head. She heard movement on the stairs as Mason pleaded with her and cursed at Richie.

Creeping as silently as she could, she felt along the wall until she came to the door of the service stairs. Trying to keep her breathing even and shallow, she turned the knob slowly, wincing when the latch clicked open.

Mason was still cursing at Richie as she closed the door behind her. Pausing in the dark, she listened and waited. Feeling the air around her, she waited. The house hadn't warned her. She longed for the sound of a slamming door to prove herself wrong.

A hiss sounded in her ear. *"You can't hide bitchhhhh."*

Covering her mouth with her hand, she sat on the top stair trying not to panic. Serena's fingers slid over the slick surface of the narrow wooden staircase. Glad of the hours she had spent lovingly sanding and varnishing the staircase herself, she knew there'd be no splinters. The pitch black seemed endless as she slowly felt each step and slid her body down. She tried counting them, but the dark was overwhelming. Mason's muffled ravings seemed so far away. She felt the wood beneath her vibrate with a strange energy. Finally, her foot came against the closed door to the kitchen. She reached for the knob and a spark of electricity shocked her. Still feeling the tingle of it, she tried again this time succeeding. The gust of cool air that greeted her was welcomed after the closeted heat of the stairwell.

Crouching by the door, she listened for movement. The kitchen was quiet except for her breathing. Mason's angry voice still seemed to be coming from the staircase.

Her heart pounding, she thought frantically of her options. She could leave out of the back door. The easiest route. The only problem was her keys still sat on the entryway table where she had left them. The extra set she kept in a drawer here in the kitchen was promptly moved after the horrible night Richie had shown up. Dragging a battered and bruised Claire, he had forced himself into her home in search of a secret stash of money. Not ever wanting to repeat the search for the extra set of keys, she had safely tucked them away in her office. Groaning inwardly, she knew it would be easier to get to the keys in the foyer. Her bare feet moved silently over the wooden floor. The odd hum continued. Taking a deep breath, she crept closer to the kitchen entryway. Mason's angry voice demanded for Richie to leave. The odd hum followed. If she stayed low and quiet maybe Mason wouldn't notice her.

On hands and knees Serena crawled in the darkness, using her hands to feel in front of her. The table was closer to the door. If she were able to grab the keys she could make a run for it.

"You need to leave Richie!" Mason threatened.

An angry hiss seemed to emerge from the humming, "*She took my money.*"

"She doesn't have your money!"

Her hand touched the table leg. Kneeling she made her way up the table to feel for the keys. The lights flickered and the strange hum grew louder in her ears.

"*Bitch, where's my money?*" A rotten smell invaded her nostrils, and the hiss encircled her. As her fingertip touched the keys, they flew from the table into the darkness crashing to the floor.

Her anger rose as she stood.

"You're dead, Richie! Don't you remember falling down the stairs. The knife. You're dead. The police have your money!"

The lights blinked wildly, the humming shook the floorboards beneath her feet.

"*No, you lie. You pushed me!*" A shadowy form appeared on the staircase in front of Mason out stretching an arm to point a ghostly finger at Serena.

"Rena, stop," Mason warned never taking his eyes from the shadow.

"No, he's dead. He needs to leave. This is my house!" Her voice echoed off the ceiling.

The shadow lunged at Mason to shove him out of the way, but Mason pushed back. The air crackled with electricity. Serena watched in disbelief as Mason struggled with the specter.

"You're dead, Richie," Mason spat through clenched teeth. "I won't let you hurt her."

In the strobing light, Serena watched in horror as Mason's foot slipped from the step and he tumbled in slow motion taking the shadowy form with him.

"No! Mason!" Her warning was pointless.

Racing to where Mason landed on the bottom step, she knelt next to him. Richie looked down at them oddly, as he floated just above Mason. He hovered, stretching out his arms. Serena felt his panic as his wraithlike form kicked to reach the floor. Not connected with anything, his movements became more frantic. His form began to expand and thin becoming more transparent.

With one last raspy scream, the house vibrated and shuddered. The lights flickered wildly as Richie completely dissolved.

Serena held on to Mason, waiting for it to pass. The house finally fell silent and she was plunged into darkness again.

"Mason," she whispered shaking his shoulder gently. "Can you hear me?"

Her hands caressed his face in the darkness. His skin was ice cold.

The front door opened letting in a dim stream of light. A deep voice inquired hesitantly, "Hello?"

"Call 911," Serena pleaded.

"Rena is that you?"

Recognizing the voice as Mason's brother's she sighed with relief. "Gabe, Mason's hurt. Please call for help."

A light shone on her, and she shielded her eyes against it.

"He's here." Motioning towards Mason, she squinted against the light. Her gaze followed the beam of light until it found Mason.

Serena let out a gasp, Mason's face was extremely pale and his lips had a strange blue tinge.

"Oh, Mason."

CHAPTER 27

By the time Serena heard the wailing of the ambulance, she had covered Mason to warm him up and dressed herself. Gabe had retrieved a flashlight from his truck and quietly wandered around the darkened house. Sitting next to Mason on the floor, she held his hand.

Evan showed up just as the EMT's were unloading the gurney. His dark eyes rounded in shock, then narrowed on Serena. "Serena, what happened?"

"Evan, don't look at me like that." Tired of suspicious looks, Serena dropped her shoulders and tried to explain. No one would believe he battled a ghost and won. "He fell down the stairs. I don't know. The lights were flickering and he fell."

"Who are you?" Noticing Gabe, Evan flashed the stream of light in his direction.

"Mason's brother, Gabriel Del Toro. Who are you?" Gabe pointed his own light in Evan's direction.

"Deputy Bertrand. Were you here?" Evan's tone took an authoritative timbre.

"No, I didn't see him fall, but the lights were flashing when I drove up." Leaning against the wall, Gabe remained relaxed and unintimidated.

"Excuse me, ma'am. You need to let us get to him." The young EMT intent on his business motioned for Serena to move away from Mason.

Reluctantly, Serena let go of Mason's hand and stood back to give them room.

"Ok, you two stay here. I'll go check the breaker." Evan pointed his flashlight in the direction of the kitchen. "Anybody else here?"

"No, it's just us." The house felt empty and cold. Serena worried over the significance of that as the EMT knelt next to Mason moving the blanket aside.

He felt for a pulse on Mason's throat, while his other hand gently slid under his neck to support it. Looking back at his partner, he shook his head.

"No. It's there." Serena moved to reach Mason again.

"Ma'am please. Just give us a minute." The older EMT gently moved Serena toward the door then kneeling next to Mason he checked again.

"He's alive. I felt his heartbeat," Serena maintained. She could feel him from where she stood.

"Yeah, maybe so." The senior EMT gave Serena a curt nod, then added, "Real faint, but it's there."

"He's alive," she repeated.

"Let's get him collared and on a board." The older man motioned to his partner.

"You don't leave here without me," Serena said firmly.

"Hey, your breaker box is a mess. You're probably going to have to replace the whole thing." Evan entered the foyer, his flashlight bouncing a ray of light along the floor. When it hit the gurney, it stopped. "Is he ok?"

"He's not responding. From the blue around his lips, it's looking like a possible electric shock. We need to get his spine secured then put him on a heart monitor. Then we'll roll to the ER."

Evan blinked at the news, then frowned in Serena's direction. They watched as the first responders secured Mason's neck with some kind of plastic collar, gently rolled him onto a board and strapped him down. Then they drew the gurney up and quickly lifted him onto it with sure, practiced hands.

Serena followed the EMT's out to the porch. Knowing Evan, he probably had more questions, but she wasn't letting Mason out of her sight until she knew he'd be ok. Another cruiser pulled up and out popped Eva like a demented jack in the box.

"Oh my god, what happened?" Eva shrieked at the sight of Mason on the gurney.

"Whoa." Walking to meet the car, Evan held out a hand. "What are you doing here?"

"Evan, remove her from my property. She's trespassing and I've already warned her." Serena could feel the anger building like a tidal wave.

"She's filed a complaint. I thought I'd take her down here and see if they can work it out." The large deputy that exited the car spoke directly to Evan.

"Hersh," Evan sighed heavily. "She doesn't belong here."

"She did this. I want to see Mason," Eva demanded.

"Are you a relative?" The older EMT asked cautiously, looking to Evan for direction.

"Yes." Lifting her pointy nose in the air, Eva straightened her back confidently.

"No, Eva, you are not." Making his presence known, Gabe moved off the porch to stand next to Serena. "You don't belong here. I had a long talk with Mason and Ben today. You have no business here."

"Well, she's not family either." The red head pointed a finger in Serena's direction.

"Eva, let the deputy take you back to where it is you came from and we'll discuss this tomorrow." Hands in his pockets, Gabe remained unflustered.

"No, she's not what she says she is. You can't believe her," Eva tried to speak around the deputy that now blocked her view.

"Ma'am, please. Get back in the car."

Serena stood next to the gurney and took Mason's hand. "He's my husband."

"That's a lie!" Eva shouted, red splotches growing on her face.

Losing patience, Gabe walked toward Eva with a menacing gaze. "You know, Eva. I'd love to hear how you got your hands on our private files. I'm sure these fine deputies would be interested in that story as well. Serena will be filing her own complaint. This is harassment."

"No, someone pushed me down the stairs."

"There were three witnesses that say you were

the only one on the stairs, and you were trespassing on private property," Gabe reminded her.

"Miss Tremaine, you never said you were here without permission."

"Whha... Umm... No." Frazzled now, Eva stomped her foot in aggravation.

"Please return to the car ma'am and I'll take you back to the station." Hersh frowned at her disapprovingly.

"Mrs. Del Toro, we need to get him to the hospital to see if there's any internal damage." The younger EMT held the gurney ready to lift it into the ambulance.

"Yes, of course." She looked down at Mason's hand in hers. It was already a little warmer.

"Don't worry. I'll follow the ambulance." Patting her shoulder, Gabe handed over the keys she had been so desperate to get her hands on earlier. "Found them on the floor."

"If you want to ride up front, it may be more comfortable." The older EMT suggested as the younger one slid into the driver's seat.

"No, I'd rather stay with him."

"Ok, if you want, but if there's complications I'll need you to stay out of the way."

Serena nodded her head and climbed in to sit next to the gurney immediately reaching for Mason's hand again. Definitely warmer.

"Hey, look at that." The EMT pointed to the monitor smiling broadly. "You brought his heart rate up, just like magic."

"Yes, it's magic," Serena whispered to herself closing her eyes against the tears. Tomorrow she knew there would be more questions than she was comfortable answering. If Mason knew about Graham, then so did everyone else. Gabriel hadn't mentioned it, but she had felt him watching her. From the look on Evan's face, he was probably questioning the similarities to the night Richie died. Eva was bound and determined to cause trouble, and now she had electrical problems. As bad as all of that sounded, her main concern lay unresponsive on the gurney next to her. She could feel his heartbeat strengthening. She didn't need a monitor to tell her that. The memory haunted her. If it were real... No, she couldn't think about that right now. Now all she could do was be grateful for their magic and the knowledge that he would be fine.

Far off voices drifted around Mason. The feeling in his body was only a tingle. His body felt like something foreign, a weight holding him down. Unable to move, he rested and listened to the voices.

"Tell me what happened." The deep voice sounded so familiar, but he couldn't place it.

"I don't know. I saw him fall, but the lights were going nuts. There was this awful humming sound." Mi Amor. He would know her anywhere. She sounded upset. He tried to move again.

"What are you doing here Gabe? I mean, not here, but in Cypress Point. Did Mason tell you everything?" Her voice sounded almost frightened.

"He gave me the files on your house. He was extremely upset about Eva getting a hold of them. I figured I'd come to help and make sure he didn't lose his head." His brother, Gabriel, always taking charge.

"That awful woman." A bit of fire in her voice now reassured him.

Gabe's chuckle was heartfelt. "Don't worry about her. I'll take care of it."

"Thank you. So you read the files?"

"Yes, I did. I tried calling Mason. He didn't answer. So I called Ben to clarify a few things. Interesting stuff."

"I know you don't believe." Her soft touch stroked Mason's hand then held it tightly.

"No I don't, but if things are that out of hand, why on earth didn't someone call me?" Just like Gabe to think he had all the answers.

"Because you don't believe," Serena answered simply, then added, "And what could you do?"

"I can't explain everything, but I think you have some sort of electrical problem with the wiring. It's an old house. I'll call someone out to check on it." His brother's voice moved around the room as he spoke. Mason knew he was pacing.

"Ben will want pictures."

"He's coming back as soon as the shoot is done." Gabe's voice came from the far side of the room.

"He knows?" Her hand tightened on his and Mason heard her gulp.

"I called him to chew him out earlier about keeping me in the dark. He was planning to come back anyway when I told him how upset Mason was. Then I called again a few minutes ago. He wanted to come straight away, but I told him the doctor said he should be fine."

"Yes, he's going to be fine."

"He will," Gabe agreed his voice closer now. "The tests are just to be sure there was no internal damage."

Mason fought to open his eyes. He couldn't quite manage more than a slit but the fuzzy shapes before him didn't move. He tried to squeeze Serena's hand, willing his fingers to curl around hers. After what seemed like an eternity, his hand gripped hers gently.

"Mason?" Serena moved closer to him. Her golden light warming him.

He wanted to speak, to tell her he was fine, but all he could manage was a slight part in his dry lips. His mouth felt like it was filled with sand as he tried again. "Re...Re..."

"Wait, hun. Here, try some water first." The fuzzy shape moved away from the bed then came nearer again pressing a straw to his lips. "Take a sip. Just go slow."

Water never tasted so good to him. It cooled his mouth and soothed his dry throat. After the first sip he tried again, this time taking a longer pull. His body seemed to be soaking it in as fast as he could drink.

"Mace, not too fast," Gabe warned.

The more he drank the more movement he could feel in his jaw.

"Better?" Serena's face came into focus slowly.

He needed to see her face and to know she wasn't frightened of him. She had to know he never meant to hurt her. Feeling with his fingers, he tried to find her hand again. "Rena."

"I'm right here, hun." Her soft hand slipped into his.

"I'm so sorry." His voice no more than a raspy whisper, Mason clung to her hand tightly.

"Mason." Her face came into view as she leaned closer to him. "Stop, Mace. Everything's going to be fine."

"Hey, Mace." Gabe's voice came even closer to the bed. Mason's eyes were able to focus enough to see the concern on his brother's face.

"Gabriel, don't call Mom," he croaked out.

"No, I didn't. The doctor just wants to run some tests but you'll be fine in a few days. I knew you wouldn't want to worry her."

"No."

"Here take another sip." Serena offered him the straw again.

"Mason do you remember what happened?" Leaning over the bed, Gabe watched him intently.

Flashes of Serena running from him up the stairs ran through his mind. The fear on her face made him wince. Then he remembered Richie appearing before him.

"Richie. He's gone. He won't bother you anymore," he spoke to Serena to reassure her.

"I saw." She smiled at him sadly. "Thank you."

"Richie? The picture of the shadow on the stairs? He did this?" Gabe backed away, rolling his eyes in disbelief.

"But he's gone now." Mason's voice grew stronger.

"That's a relief." Serena sighed focusing on Mason. "Why don't you just rest now and we can talk more about that later?"

"That's a good idea," Gabe agreed with a nod. "Rena, let me take you home so you can get some rest, too. It's been a long night for everyone."

"No, you go ahead. I'll give you my keys." Serena seemed reluctant to leave him and that gave him hope.

"No, love, go with Gabe. I'll be fine." He squeezed her hand again. "Just promise me you'll be there when I get out."

"Of course. It's my home. I'm not going anywhere."

CHAPTER 28

Gabriel was quiet on the drive home. Serena watched the sky lighten, waiting for his questions about Graham, the house, and Mason's injury. She knew he'd be looking for logical explanations for events happening at Coeur du Bayou. She wouldn't argue with him. Let him find answers that made him feel better. She knew. Mason had confirmed what she had seen with her own eyes. Richie was gone. Claire and Evan could proceed with their wedding plans without fear of Richie making an appearance.

Her sigh of relief made Gabe glance her way as he navigated the long driveway to Coeur du Bayou.

"Glad to be home?"

"Yes, with one less spirit in the house." Serena smiled at him waiting for the eye roll. Instead she was rewarded with a thoughtful nod.

"It's going to be hot in there. I've got to call someone about the electricity as soon as possible. I'll open some windows." She was surprised to see Faith on the porch. Gabe started to say something, but she was out of the truck before he had fully stopped.

"What happened?" Faith's hand went to her hip. "The electricity is off. I can't bake."

"You haven't talked to Evan?"

"No, why? What's wrong?"

"Well, the good news… Richie is gone." Serena stopped on the steps of the porch to let the news sink in. He was gone.

"Wow! Ok, but…" Hands still on her hips, Faith waited for an explanation.

"The bad news. Mason is in the hospital and the electricity is fried." Before Faith could react Serena added, "I'm going to call and see if I can get someone out here to fix it."

"Is Mason ok?" Faith asked, her hands falling to her sides.

"Yes, they said he'd be fine in a day or two." Serena tried to reassure her with a smile but she was so exhausted her face felt numb.

"Oh…" Faith finally noticed Gabe as he approached the steps.

"Sorry. Faith, this is Mason's brother, Gabriel Del Toro."

"Hi." Faith smiled uncomfortably.

"Let's go in. I'm sure it's smothering in there." Motioning to the door, Serena tried to avoid an awkward silence.

"Not too bad yet." Faith led the way into the foyer.

"Gabe, I'll put you in a room upstairs, if you want. I'm sure it'll be sticky until I can get someone out here."

"Don't worry about that. I'll take care of it," he said simply.

"What do you mean?"

"Serena, let me do this for you. I tried to tell you in the truck, but you were anxious to get out. I'll have someone out here in a few hours and depending on the damage, hopefully we'll be sleeping in the AC tonight." Gabe started up the stairs.

"You think you can have someone out here that quick?" Serena had figured the best she could hope for was a few days.

"I know. I've already called in a favor. I'll take pictures if Ben doesn't make it back in time," Gabe said over his shoulder as he continued up the stairs.

"Ok."

"Just get some rest, if you can." He smirked at her.

"Faith, I'll call you when it's back on." Serena turned to Faith, too exhausted to have a long conversation.

"Yeah. Ok." Faith was watching Gabe as he made his way to the landing. "Not the yellow one in the front, ok?"

"Not the yellow room, ok." He nodded curtly to them.

"It's Anna's room. You don't want to go in there." Faith twisted her hands then rubbed them on her jeans.

"It's ok, Faith."

After Gabe disappeared into the only other available room, Faith whispered to Serena, "He was looking at me funny."

"What? I don't think so. We're so tired. We were at the hospital all night. I'm sure he's exhausted too."

Serena walked back out onto the porch with Faith. The sun was higher now, already warming everything it touched.

"Yeah. I'm sorry about Mason, but I know Claire will be relieved."

"I figure Evan will be thrilled."

"Yeah, so the wedding? We can really start moving things along now." Faith raised her eyebrows and gave Serena a smile.

"Yes, let me get the house back running and we can finalize the plans."

Faith's gaze locked on the Coeur du Bayou sign. Reaching a hand out, she traced the lettering with a fingertip.

"He loved me," she whispered.

"What?"

"He loved me. He made this sign for me." Dazed, Faith caressed the dainty painted flowers with her fingers.

"Faith, are you ok?"

"My father, when he found out…" She shook her head sadly. "He was so angry. He was going to burn this sign. I found it in the burn pile out back, I hid it from him. It's the only thing I had left of Jacques."

"Are you remembering this now?" Serena whispered.

Faith blinked rapidly. "Um. No. I saw it before."

"So that's why it was stuck in the back of the

closet. Anna hid it from her father." Serena smiled at the simple explanation and marveled at how it had stayed hidden for so long.

"Yeah. I got to go. I can't bake so I'll go to the diner and help Gil." Suddenly in a hurry, Faith made her way to her car.

"I'll call you," Serena called to Faith as she climbed in and slammed the door.

"What's going on?" Gabe asked from the staircase.

"Faith's leaving and I'm going to bed." Serena closed the heavy door behind her and sagged against it. The heat would make it nearly impossible to sleep.

"Just wanted to let you know, the electrician is on his way."

"Great."

"Is everything alright? I thought you'd be more relieved about the Richie guy being gone."

"I'm just worried about Faith. She's so obsessed with Anna." Pushing herself away from the door, Serena felt the sweat already pooling on her lower back.

"Oh, right. The ghost lady." There was the eye roll she had expected earlier.

"I'm too tired to argue with you right now." Serena waved a limp hand at him.

Gabe gave a small laugh and looked around curiously. "Get some rest. Maybe when you wake up everything will be back to normal. It'll be like a bad dream."

"Gabe, that would be magic."

Waking to the sounds of male voices in her house, Serena was momentarily startled until it all came back to her. Her sweat soaked skin and the heavy stale air let her know the house was still without electricity.

Sneaking upstairs, she took a quick cold shower in the hopes that it would revive her long enough to sort out what needed to be done. Gabe had been helpful, but he didn't believe. He'd be looking for logical answers, facts or not. Ben would be back soon, miffed that he missed all the action. At least she'd have a few days before she had to deal with Mason and the memories.

Immediately feeling guilty, Serena needed to check in on him. She knew she wouldn't leave him in the hospital alone. As she dressed, she made plans to drive back over. If Ben made it back in time, he'd probably go with her.

Making her way back downstairs she heard Gabe's voice. "So you think it was faulty wiring?"

"I can't explain it. That's the only thing I can think of and don't ask me how your brother connected with it from the staircase." The other male voice sounded thoroughly mystified.

Serena smiled at Gabe's attempt to find the cause. Catching a reflection of light through the sidelight, she made her way to the front door. Seeing Ben's Land Rover parked in the driveway, she made her way back to the kitchen as Gabe was coming out.

"Hey. Ben's here. I was thinking of going back to the hospital. I'm sure Ben's going to want to come too," Serena gave him a hopeful look then added, "if you have this covered."

"It should be fixed by nightfall, but don't bother going back up there."

"Why?"

The front door opened and Ben came in holding it wide. "You sure you don't need help?"

"Reuben," Mason's voice was weak but firm as he stepped over the threshold. "I'm just moving a little slow."

"Mason." Serena hurried over to the door as Mason held on to the door jamb. "What are you doing?"

"He called me. I was planning to go by there anyway, but when I got there he promptly checked himself out." Ben frowned in Mason's direction.

"You should have stayed until you were stronger."

"And miss all the fun?" Mason's breath was labored as he looked around the room. "God, it's hot in here."

"Let's get you to your room."

"No, I need to sit for a minute." He pointed to the parlor then took a shaky step.

"All right, stop being stubborn." Ben put an arm around Mason's waist and helped him to the nearest chair. "Ok, if you're good, I'm going to get some pictures and check equipment."

"You go on ahead. I'll just sit right here."

The paleness of his face and the sheen of sweat over his lip worried Serena. "Mason, you should have stayed at the hospital until you were stronger."

"Ah, love… Worried about me still?" There was hope in his voice as he gazed at her longingly.

"Of course." Serena lowered her eyes unable to meet his.

"I had to make sure he was gone. I don't feel him. No trace."

"No, I don't either. I saw him leave." Her eyes

wandered to the mantle and her neatly placed candlesticks.

"I had to make sure you were safe."

"I am. I'm home."

"Are we not going to talk about it?"

"Mace, please. I think we should wait till you're feeling better. It'll give me more time to process everything. This heat is not helping."

"Faulty wiring? Are you kidding me?" Ben's exasperated voice rose as he entered the parlor. "Here's water for everyone. Two for Mason. Got to keep hydrated."

Gabe followed him in not ready to give up his argument. "The electrician said it's the only logical explanation."

"I guess it's too much to hope that you left video running on the stairs?" Mason asked his eyes fixed on the water bottles. Serena held her breath, knowing that Richie wouldn't have been the only thing to see on the stairs. Whatever was between them, madness or magic, it was private.

"No, I thought I'd be gone a few days and I didn't want Serena to have to worry about batteries. With Faith in and out of here, I didn't think it was a good idea."

"Speaking of Faith, I'm really worried about her. I was going to wait until Mason was feeling better." Serena twisted the cap off the bottle then twisted it back on.

"What's wrong?"

"Mace, do you feel Anna here?" Finally looking at him, Serena hoped his answer wouldn't confirm her fears.

"Ummm. Sadness. It's still there. Burnt smell."

"Could the burnt smell have been a premonition of what was going to happen?" Ben asked curiously.

"Maybe, but I still smell it."

"I don't smell anything." Gabe sniffed the air around him.

"No, I don't feel Anna." Mason sat straighter in his chair. "Why are you asking?"

"She didn't warn me about Richie last night. I thought maybe she was gone, too."

"Well, isn't that the goal?" Gabe frowned at her.

"Yes, but Faith had a really bad episode yesterday, and not in the house."

"Whoa... Wow. You're right," Ben said excitedly. "It was in the graveyard."

"So, you're thinking..." Mason put a bottle to his forehead and closed his eyes.

"Anna's hitched a ride with Faith," Ben answered for her.

"She was upset that the electricity wasn't on this morning. At first I thought it was because she couldn't bake, but at the door she got weird. She told me about the sign and how she hid it in the upstairs closet, but it was from Anna's point of view."

"That's crazy. Should we get her back over here?" Blue eyes wide, Ben paced in front of the mantle, his shirt already damp with sweat.

"Yes, we need to do another session," Mason agreed.

"When you're stronger and the electricity is back on." Serena wasn't sure it was the best course of action, but something needed to be done.

"They're putting the new box in now. Shouldn't be much longer." Gabe rubbed his eyes, sitting heavily on the loveseat.

"Yeah, I need to check all of my equipment. Ugh. The batteries are probably going to have to be replaced." Ben frowned and headed out of the room. "The new batteries might have been drained, too."

"It certainly felt like it." Mason gave a halfhearted laugh.

CHAPTER 29

Grateful for the hum of electricity coursing through Coeur du Bayou, Serena breathed in the cool air. Mason was looking better every day and moving around more. She knew he wanted to talk about the memories, but she wasn't ready. His eyes followed her everywhere. She felt his regret and it saddened her.

Wanting to give him time to recover, she had kept her distance. Actually she was afraid the memory would return. How could they be together, constantly reliving that horrible memory?

Pushing it from her mind, she tried to focus on the task at hand. Faith. Her behavior was becoming stranger every time she came by. Mason had insisted on another session. Bringing more water bottles upstairs, she passed one to Ben as he grumbled over his video recorder in the pale yellow room.

"So you're telling me she ended up marrying the Harold guy?" Mason asked Ben but his eyes were on Serena. Happy to see his coloring was back to normal, she smiled at him.

"Yes, it all came together quickly once I figured out the name. The first mayor of Cypress Point was John Bertrand. His son, Harold married Anna Fox in 1905," Ben recalled from memory.

"I still can't believe it." Serena shook her head frowning. It didn't make sense.

"The other graves out there are her parents, Harold, and I'm assuming other relatives. Haven't connected all of them yet." Fresh batteries inserted, he snapped the cover back on the video camera.

"Well, it gives me a new line of questioning." Mason flipped through the papers in the file. "I think we should start with the baby and go from there. Maybe if we take some of the focus off of Jacques, she'll tell us more about the baby."

"Yeah, I think so," Ben agreed.

"Wait. Bertrand?" Serena leaned over Mason to see the file. "Any relation to Faith?"

"Faith?" Mason gave her a confused look.

"Oh, my. This is crazy. Could Faith and Evan be descendants of Anna?" Serena wondered out loud.

"That would be too much of a coincidence, wouldn't it?" Gabe said from the doorway.

"I don't want to ask Faith. She's already kinda..." Ben circled a finger around his temple.

"No, I think you should talk to Evan." Serena saw his grimace, then suggested, "Or Margaret."

Ben gave her a blank look.

"Margaret, their mom. She'd be happy to talk to you."

"Umm, yeah. I remember her from the engagement party." A panicked look crossed Ben's face.

"Ben, she's an awesome cook," Serena teased him. "Where do you think Faith learned to cook?"

"Ok, I'll go talk to her." Ben rubbed his stomach grinning. "Maybe around lunch time."

"Mason, are you sure you're up for this?"

"Sure, love." His smile didn't quite reach his eyes. She knew she was the cause and the remedy. Soon, she'd have to find a way to make things right.

At the sound of the door opening downstairs, Gabe stuck his head over the railing and called out to Faith, "We're up here."

Mason closed the file, handing it to Serena to put away.

Faith gave Gabriel a wary glance as she passed him in the doorway of Anna's room. Going directly to the bed, she laid back without a word.

"Everything ok, Faith?"

"Yeah." She lifted her head to look at Mason. "Are you sure Jake shouldn't be here?"

"No, it's better if he's not. That way if we do another session with him we'll know if he's actually remembering instead of just recalling information from your sessions."

"Oh, yeah. I guess that makes sense."

"Why don't you just get comfortable? Rena brought up some water, if you need it."

"Ok." Faith leaned back on the bed and closed her eyes.

"Gabe, stay or go, but close the door."

"I think I'll stay." Gabe closed the door and stood behind Mason leaning comfortably against the wall.

"Ben. Ready?" Mason waited for Ben's confirmation.

"Yep. We're a go." Ben gave a thumbs up.

"Rena, maybe you should move away from the door." Mason's concern was apparent but she wasn't moving away from the door. If it opened she planned to stand between it and Mason.

"I'm good."

"Ok, let's get started." He gave them a nod, then softened his voice. "Just relax, Faith. Breath in and out... Listen to the sound of my voice..."

"I'm here." An impatient voice came from Faith.

Mason blinked, speaking softly, "Anna?"

"Yes. I don't know where Jacques's buried. I've searched and searched. I wanted him next to me." Anna's speech tumbled from Faith as if she'd been waiting a long time to speak.

"Anna, I know you loved him."

"I did. We were supposed to get married."

"So what happened? Can you tell me?"

"My father killed him. He killed him and dragged him into the woods. I don't know where." Her soft cries filled the room.

"Anna, I'm sorry. The baby. What about the baby?"

"My baby. I don't know where she is either." The crying continued.

"You were pregnant?"

"Yes, he wanted to marry me." Faith's hands cradled her stomach.

"But your father wanted you to marry Harold?"

"Yes, he told me I had to get rid of the baby." The anger in her voice was unmistakable.

"Anna, what did you do?"

"I told him I wanted my baby. I begged him, but he put me on a boat to New Orleans till I had the baby."

"Did you have the baby?"

"Yes, my little girl. They took her from me!" Her voice rose in desperation. "I hate him. I swore he'd be sorry."

"Did you come back here after?"

"Yes, he made me marry Harold. He owed money and was going to lose the lumber mill if the gambling boat didn't come."

"Oh. The mayor was Harold's father and he needed his help to get the boat here."

"Yes, but it didn't work out. I made sure of that."

"What happened? What did you do?"

"I wanted to make sure he was ruined. I burned down the lumber yard."

"What?" Mason's expression changed from concern to surprise.

"I begged him to let me have my baby back. I said I'd marry anyone he wanted me to, if I could have my baby. He said no one would want me if they knew." She turned towards Mason, her eyes flashing with anger. "But he did. Jacques wanted me and my baby."

The door flung open suddenly. Gabe stepped out to look down the hallway. Serena grabbed him, pushing him back into the room clear of the door. Standing in front of Mason, she waited for it to slam shut.

"Anna, calm down please," Mason tried to reassure her. The bedroom door slammed shut making Gabe start.

"No! He did it."

A gust of wind blew the door open again, bouncing it against the wall.

"No, Poppa, no!" Anna screamed as the house began to shake. Grabbing his head, Mason began to moan.

"No. Mason wake her up," Serena whispered to Mason watching the door way. When Mason didn't answer she pleaded, "Faith, wake up."

Mason began to fall forward limply. Gabe caught his shoulders to keep him from falling out of the chair. Faith began to scream, writhing on the bed in jerky motions. Serena frantically tried to recall the safe word.

"The word, Ben. What's the word?"

"There was no word." Stumped, Ben shook his head.

She thought back to the last session, their dance and Mason's promise.

"J'adoube! J'adoube!"

Faith fell back on the bed as the house shuddered. Eerie moaning continued around them.

"*My baby.*" A soft whimper made the hairs on the back of her neck stand up.

"Mason. Mason." Gabe shook Mason by his shoulders roughly.

"Gabe. Stop." Mason slapped at his brother's hands trying to break free of his grip.

"Are you ok?" Serena knelt next to him.

"Yeah. I think." He glanced at Faith on the bed.

"Get her out of here."

"What?"

"Don't you feel it? Anna's back in the house. Get Faith out before she decides to hitch a ride again."

"Faith. Can you hear me?" Standing to lean over the bed, Serena shook Faith's shoulder urgently.

"Noooo. Stop," Faith moaned opening her eyes. "It was bad. Oh God. Serena, she was so mad." Her death grip on the bed spread twisted it as she sat up slowly.

"It's ok. Here, let's get you downstairs out on the porch. Maybe some fresh air will help." Serena tried to pull her off of the bed.

"She did it." Faith grabbed her arm and pulled her closer.

"What? What did she do?"

"She killed her father," Faith whispered loudly, gripping her arm tighter.

"I know, Faith. I saw it." Mason patted her hand. "It's over now."

"What did you see?" Ben asked from the corner, adjusting the camera on Mason.

"The lumber yard on fire. The burnt smell. That's why I kept smelling it. Her father was there when she started the fire." He exhaled fully, sitting back against the chair obviously drained.

"Oh, wow. Yeah. I saw something about that. Hang on." Ben pulled out the file again and flipped through the pages.

"Mason, drink some water," Gabe ordered, shoving a water bottle in his face.

"I'm fine." Mason pushed it away and rubbed his face.

"You don't look fine." His brother dropped the

bottle in Mason's lap.

"I'm just tired." Mason rubbed his face again.

"We should have waited." Serena was at a loss for words. Anna had seemed so innocent, but Serena knew love made people do crazy things.

"Here it is," Ben spoke up. "The lumber mill burned in 1905. It nearly took out the whole town. The owner Leland Fox perished in the fire, presumably trying to put it out."

"But she knew he was there." Faith looked to Mason. "Right?"

"Yes, she knew." The sadness in Mason's green-gold eyes was unbearable.

"I've got to go." Letting go of Serena, Faith pushed herself up off of the bed.

"Should I call Jake or drive you home?" Worried about her friend, Serena hated to let her go off alone.

"No," Faith snapped. "Maybe he shouldn't be here."

Bewildered by the change in Faith's attitude, Serena watched her closely. Faith took one last look around the yellow room then quickly turned on her heel exiting the room with a flip of her ponytail.

"Gabe, please help Mason to his room. I'll walk Faith out," Serena said before hurrying out of the room after Faith. "You sure you're ok?"

"Yeah, I'm tired and just a little freaked out." Faith never stopped moving.

Serena followed her down the stairs. "Is there anything else you remember that might help?"

"No, just the baby. I don't think we'll ever find out what happened to it." Stopping briefly on the last step, she answered then headed for the door.

"What makes you think that?" Serena grabbed her

arm before she could swing the door open. Faith turned to face Serena, her eyes glistening with tears.

"The room she had it in. It was so dark and it was hot. I couldn't really see anything else before but today… The people in the room with her… It was nuns in the room. He sent her to a convent. If they gave it up for adoption, there might not be any record of it. You know back in those days things were different."

Standing at the door to Coeur du Bayou, Serena listened to the house. The sadness was still there, but lessened somehow. Her thoughts raced and the house warmed the chill that ran through her. She heard her grandmother's voice as clear as day, *"Careful what you wish for, girl."*

"Oh, Faith…" Eyes huge, she grabbed for her friend's hand. "I know…"

"What?"

"Listen to me. I have to make sure I'm right, but it's going to be ok."

"What are you talking about?"

"Everything. Tell Claire to send out the invitations."

The smell of gardenias enveloped them and Faith smiled.

CHAPTER 30

"Where is she?" Mason demanded. The sick feeling had returned. A dreadful panic clawed at his gut as he gripped the railing of the staircase. The episode yesterday with Faith had drained him more than he let on. Succumbing to the sleep that his body obviously needed, he had slept through the night and most of the next day. He knew immediately upon waking that she was gone.

"Mace, calm down. She said she'd be back." Ben rushed to help him down the staircase.

"Why didn't she tell me she was leaving?" He gave in, leaning on Ben to speed his progress.

"You were exhausted and finally sleeping. Even

Gabe said to let you rest." Ben groaned under his weight as they descended.

"Gabe. Where is he?" The final cursed step loomed before him. Mason held his breath and pushed forward dragging Ben with him.

"I'm down here. What's all the grumbling?" Gabe called from the parlor.

"Where is she?" Mason demanded again letting go of Ben at the parlor entrance. His momentum made his step unsure and his leg threatened to give.

"Sit down before you fall," Gabriel spoke from an arm chair, book in hand. Taking charge and making himself at home as was his way.

"I'm fine." Mason steadied himself.

"No, you are not fine. Sit."

"Fine." Mason stumbled to the love seat letting gravity pull him down to the softness of the fabric. So like Serena, the colors and fabric. There was so much of her in this house. The panic clawed at him again. "Someone please tell me where she is."

"Umm… She didn't exactly say, but I know she'll be back." Ben rubbed his back and stretched.

"You let her leave without asking where she was going?" Mason marveled at Ben's reluctance to get information, when that was something he prided himself on.

"She asked for the info I had on Anna and said there was something she needed to check on."

"What?" He tried to imagine what could have made her leave without saying goodbye. Visions of his blood soaked hand gripping the handle of a blade danced before him.

"I don't know."

"Call Faith," Mason demanded. "Does she

know?"

"Faith is in the kitchen, and she doesn't know," Gabriel informed him, his patience wearing thin.

"Faith!" Mason hollered struggling to lift himself from the soft cushion of the loveseat.

"Sit down," his brother barked at him.

"What's going on?" Faith rushed into the room wiping her discolored fingers on a towel, oblivious to the matching smears of blue on her cheek and arm.

"Where did she go?" Mason gave up and relaxed back into the overstuffed settee.

"Oh. I don't know. She told me everything's going to be fine. And it will." Nodding her head at Mason, she smiled. There was something different about her. Her nervousness was gone.

"That's it?" Mason narrowed his eyes at her, needing more information.

"No, when she said it, I felt it. Like before with the gardenias. Anna is going to make it alright."

Mason looked to his brother for help deciphering Faith's declaration.

"I don't understand it either, but I'm sure everything will be fine." Gabriel rose from his chair to pace.

"I'll call my P.I." Patience was never his thing. Mason hated waiting and he couldn't bear for her to disappear again. He had to fix this.

Gabe howled with laughter. "No, you won't. He couldn't find her in three years. I've let him go."

"What?" Stunned at his brother's arrogance, Mason blinked rapidly, trying to focus.

"He's stealing your money and he's not reliable. I've done some digging of my own."

"Gabriel. You had no right. You always have to

takeover. This isn't about you." Angry now, Mason gave in to the long buried resentments of his youth.

"Mason." His brother tried to stop his tirade.

"You don't know everything." The dreadful memory rose before him and his soul grieved.

"I know more than you think. For example, here. What's this?" Pointing to the mantle, Gabe drew their attention to the photo of Serena and Evan. It leaned against the candlestick innocently.

"Where did you get that?"

"I found it on the floor the night I got here. When the deputy was the first one on the scene I was suspicious so I just held on to it."

"That's my brother." Faith's ponytail slashed the air as she turned her dark eyes on Gabriel.

"Yes, I know that now."

"Who took that?" Faith demanded, the smear on her arm had grown with her futile attempts to wipe it away.

"Mason's P.I."

"What? You were spying on Serena?" Faith now turned to Mason. The sting of betrayal in her voice matched the expression on Ben's face.

"No," he denied the accusation.

"Exactly my point. You weren't paying him to follow Serena, so why did he take the picture?"

"Ugh. Eva."

"Yep. She obviously wanted you to think Serena and the deputy were involved." Taking the picture from the mantle, Gabe held it up as evidence.

"No, that's ridiculous." Faith shook her head as she wiped again at the coloring on her arm. "Evan was coming to meet Claire at the diner. We were inside watching through the window."

"Yes, I know."

"Then why…" Mason ran his hands through his hair, his frustration building.

"Eva thought she could get rid of Serena to get back with you and revive the show plans." Ben put the pieces together.

"That…" Still in a fog of misery, Mason struggled for words.

"Cunt!" Faith supplied for him.

Gabriel cut in, "Don't worry about her. I've taken care of it. You weren't exactly in any shape to handle things. I called our lawyer. He made a call to their family lawyer. So daddy's been alerted to the trouble she's been causing. Theft and trespassing would definitely cause some talk."

"Oh." Mason regarded his brother again. This time with admiration. "Thank you."

"She didn't get the files from me," Ben said solemnly.

"We know, Ben."

"And there's nothing going on between Serena and Evan," Faith snorted.

"We know that too. And if we pursue any investigation it won't be through that bumbling idiot. I've gotten everything he was working on for you, but if you want my opinion on what's going on with Serena, you should just ask her," Gabriel admonished, then added, "When she gets back of course."

"That doesn't help me right now." The clawing sensation returned.

"Look, she said for Claire to send out the invitations. The wedding is next month. And she was fine when we talked."

"Are you sure?" Mason wished again he had seen

Serena before she left. They never talked about the memory and he had no idea how she felt about it. She hadn't seemed frightened of him, but had clearly kept her distance.

"Yes." Faith snorted impatiently, still rubbing at the blue coloring on her arm.

"What happened between you two that night?" Through narrowed eyes, his brother watched him.

"Nothing." Damn him. He had no intention of ever telling anyone about that horrible memory.

"Ahh… the picture." Looking at the photo in his hand, Gabe grinned. "You were already in quite a state about Graham when you left home that morning."

"Graham?" Ben's surprised reaction told Mason she had kept that secret from them all.

"She's been working for him since she left us," Mason admitted. The words still burned and he hung his head in shame.

"Oh man, you didn't?" Ben groaned. Mason knew Ben was referring to his uncontrollable jealousy where Serena was concerned.

"I've apologized. We're ok. At least I hope so."

"Don't worry. She'll come back. This is her home." Blue smear still on her cheek, Faith gave a snort and stated the obvious.

Coeur du Bayou was her home. She might not come back to him, but she would come back here.

CHAPTER 31

The road stretched out before Serena. The yellow lines whizzing past her headlights had a strange calming effect on her. Reminded of her earlier travels, she thought it ironic how all of those years searching brought her right back down these roads. This time she knew she was on the road home.

Her trip had been successful but emotional. She had no one to tell. Yes, she did. And they were all waiting for her at home. Her smile widened as she chanted the word 'home'.

Coeur du Bayou. She wanted to tell Mason privately but their conversation could wait a little longer. Even he had played a part in the unraveling of the meaning of it all. They all had: Ben, Jake, Faith. Even Claire and Evan. Her family.

Family. Home. Those words were a magic balm that lifted her spirit and made the miles fly by.

Before turning onto the driveway, she stopped the car to gaze at her home, Coeur du Bayou. Jake had said it was named because of the shape of the two waterways meeting. The bayou wrapped around the property. The house, as well as the people inside it, had wrapped around her heart. The warm glow of lights in the windows told her they were there waiting. She had called Ben to ask that they all be there waiting for her. She knew Ben could be counted on not to ask too many questions, until she was ready to explain.

Admiring the lights as she parked her car, she noticed how impressive a spectacle it made. She wondered if Claire and Evan should have opted for an evening wedding. If the reception lasted long enough, the guests would see this view when departing. There would be other weddings. Many, if she had her way. Anna didn't have the wedding she wanted but she could watch over every other wedding that took place at Coeur du Bayou.

Pausing at the heavy door, she savored the moment. The expansive front porch felt solid underfoot. The large white columns stood proud and the door in front of her was strong. She knew it would always open for her.

Making her way through it, she heard voices from the parlor. Mainly Claire chattering away about the wedding plans.

"Did she say what time?" Mason's agitated voice broke into Claire's description of the crab cakes she was having catered.

"She'll be here. Stop worrying." Ben's short answer showed he was more interested in the food discussion.

She heard Mason's gasp, sensing her right before she stepped into the room. "I'm here."

"Rena." Mason stood immediately and went to her, his arms wrapping around her tightly. "Are you ok?"

"Worried about me?" She smiled slyly at him, giving him a wink.

He kissed her passionately and she couldn't help but respond. Their fire still burned brightly.

"Ok, break it up. We're here. What's going on?" Jake sat tensely on the edge of his seat next to Faith.

"Jake." Faith snorted slapping him on the knee.

"No, he's right. We're all here." Evan frowned in Gabe's direction. "What's going on?"

"It's about the wedding, right?" Claire asked excitedly. "Everything's ok?"

"The wedding will be magnificent. I promise."

"Then what?"

Serena took a deep breath, wondering how to start. Her heart filled with emotion, she began, "Umm. Everyone knows about Anna and the things that have been going on here, right?" She glanced at Gabe and Evan. "I know some of you don't want to believe. We've been trying to figure out what Anna wanted."

"The baby," Faith blurted out. "Did you find it?"

"I know what happened to it." Her dark curls bounced as she nodded to Faith. "Her father made her give it up. An orphanage ran by nuns in New Orleans. They didn't keep very accurate records of unwed mothers from wealthy families."

"Oh, what did you find?"

"My great grandmother was raised in an orphanage, given up at birth. I had some digging to do but the dates match, and it was her."

Mason's hand tightened on hers, she felt his warmth and love. Holding her breath, she waited for their reactions.

Claire moved first, her blue eyes dancing with excitement as she jumped from her seat to hug Serena. "Wow! That's amazing! Right Faith?"

"My grandmother told me stories about her mother growing up at the orphanage but I never gave it much thought. It was so long ago and it really didn't effect me."

"So Anna was your great great grandmother? That's insane." Ben whistled with appreciation.

"So you have come home!" Claire beamed.

"Yes, I have dreamed of this house all of my life and now I know why."

Ben coughed nervously. "Umm.. That's unexpected news. Weird thing though…." He ran a hand nervously through his hair. "I talked to Margaret like you asked."

"Mom?" Faith blinked at them still stunned at the news.

"What does she have to do with this?" Evan demanded.

"I just needed some family info." Ben held out his hands, not ready to take on Faith and Evan at once.

"Why?" Evan asked suspiciously, narrowing his eyes at Ben.

"Anna did marry after she gave up the baby and

the lumber mill burned. She married Harold Bertrand, and they had two children together."

"No!" Faith stood.

"One son, named after his father, Harold. Great grandfather to your dad, Edward," Ben continued.

Evan let out a groan as he pushed his dark bangs from his forehead. "We're related, kind of?"

"Yes, it would seem so." Serena smiled at the news.

"Yes!" Claire jumped up and down. "We are family, see?"

Climbing in Evans's lap she beamed happily. "And we get to be married here where it all started."

"Faith? Are you ok?" Serena noticed Faith's lack of reaction and worried she had been disappointed by the news.

"Yeah, this is weird." Her voice barely a whisper, Faith stared at the floor in shock.

"Babe, what's wrong?" Jake pulled her back down to the love seat next to him.

"I don't know. I'm just not sure what this means. For us."

"What are you talking about? That has nothing to do with us." Jake squeezed her hand.

"How can you say that? After everything. The song. The memories."

"Those memories I had are just that. It didn't even feel like me having them." Jake shrugged shaking his head at Faith.

"But…"

"No, listen to me, Faith." Taking her face in his hands, Jake made her look into his eyes. "I fell in love with you. You. Back in high school. You and me. It had nothing to do with this house. I don't know how to explain it. I'm not sure I'll ever understand any of it. But I think Anna used us to let Serena know what happened here with her baby. That's all."

She nodded silently as a tear raced down her face. Jake pulled her to him and she hid her face against his chest.

"That's a reasonable explanation. And probably as good as it's going to get," Mason agreed squeezing Serena's hand again.

"And now we can get back to my wedding plans!" The blush on Claire's face made her eyes seem bluer. "It's going to be perfect. Richie is gone and Anna found her baby."

Ben coughed again as he headed out the door. "Umm. Yeah, I've got stuff to take care of."

"Yeah, the rest of the pie," Faith snorted, lifting her face from Jake's shirt.

"I'll give you a hand with that, Reuben." Gabe laughed as he stood to follow Ben.

***

After seeing the other couples out, Serena reveled in the warmth of happiness and friendship. Smiling to herself, she mentally added family to that list. The word was magic. She leaned against the heavy door and marveled at everything that had transpired within these walls. She truly felt it had been magic all along.

Hearing a noise from the big room, she paused. The unmistakable sound of a candle being lit came through the slight crack in the sliding door. Mason. Music drifted through the air to her and she felt the pull of longing. The music, him, the memories, and the passion. Slipping through the opening, she closed the door behind her letting the soft light surround her. She knew he was waiting there in the shadows for her.

"Mi Amor." His deep husky voice reached out to her over the music.

"Mason...," she began.

"No, love, dance with me. Can we just dance?"

She went to him melting instantly against his body. No words were needed. They let the music take them, moving by feel. His strong arms held her as his muscular legs brushed against hers. The heat between them began to build and her soul rejoiced. Their energy melded and flowed with the music.

When the song ended, Serena couldn't bear to open her eyes. She just wanted to feel. Not think. Not remember.

"Rena, my love." His strong hand caressed her back and found its way under her chin lightly turning her face upward. She opened her eyes then to see his green gold ones watching her intently. "Can you ever forgive me?"

"Mason, you came back for me. You came back to make things right and you did. Our magic is real." Reaching up to softly kiss him on the lips, she watched his eyes close on unshed tears. She felt his relief as he crushed her to him.

"I love you," she whispered into his lips. "We are bound."

CHAPTER 32

Coeur du Bayou was bustling with activity and Serena loved every minute of it. Noisy clattering from the kitchen told her Faith was busy in her domain. Upstairs, Michelle was setting up for the last fitting before the rehearsal supper. The big room was set and ready for the guests. Finally deciding that the room needed a more formal title, Serena had dubbed it, 'The Event Room', and she had every intention of it earning the name. Noticing Ben lurking in the foyer near the boxed desserts for the reception, Serena quietly watched as he sneaked a mini pie out of the pastry box.

"Ben! What are you doing?"

Looking guiltily at the treat in his hand, he smiled quickly and replied, "Quality assurance."

"Faith is going to kill you if you don't stay out of the food. Those are for the reception tomorrow."

"Then why are they out?"

"Gil's coming to pick these up to store at the diner until tomorrow. And they were boxed." Serena pointed to the stack of boxes that were closed and taped.

"I'm here!" A frazzled Elle burst into the foyer, pushing her sunglasses over her spiky hair.

"Elle, it's ok. You're not late. Relax." Serena smiled at her.

"Oh, good. Am I staying here tonight?"

"Well, I don't know. I thought you were staying at your mom's."

"Elle." Ben nodded in her direction awkwardly.

"Hey," Elle answered shyly, and lowered her voice in Serena's direction. "Hey, you think you have time to do a reading for me? I think I need it."

"What?" Taken aback by the request, Serena didn't have time to answer before the door opened again.

"Elle. What the hell?" Evan strode in carrying a bag. "You're only here for a few days. Your car looks like you've got your whole house in it, and you've been living in it."

"Evan, what are you doing here? We have to try on the dresses. You shouldn't be here."

He pointed to the door as Claire entered. "Hey, I thought it'd be better if he just dropped me off now, instead of taking two cars."

Evan turned back to his sister with a frown. "I'm not hauling all that down. You don't need it."

"No, that doesn't get unloaded here. It's going to Claire's." Elle's smile faded, and she bit the side of her lip. "I guess she hasn't told you."

"Told me what?" Evan looked from Elle to Claire then back at his sister for an explanation.

"I'm moving back. Claire's going to rent me her house." The diamond stud glinted from the side of her nose as she gave a cheesy smile to her brother.

After a few blinks, he asked, "What about your job?"

Elle's smile faded as she looked at her sandals. "Umm... I quit."

"Has that hair dye gone to your brain?"

"Evan." Claire smacked him on the arm.

"Why did you quit Elle?" Serena asked, realizing her request for the reading. "Are you ok?"

"No, damn it. I'm not ok!" Elle's cheeks grew red as she stomped a foot on the wood floor. "Claire told me what happened and I missed it. All of it."

"Oh man," Ben grumbled, looking at the half eaten dessert in his hand.

"What the hell are you going to do here?" Evan demanded.

"I'll find another job. I just don't want to miss anything else." Her large brown eyes threatened to water. "Everyone I love is here."

Evan blinked again, nodded silently and cleared his throat. "Where's Faith?"

"In the kitchen finishing up the cake. And don't go in there. I stuck my head in and I thought she was going to stab me." Ben rolled his eyes toward the kitchen and popped the last bite into this mouth.

Claire blushed with happiness as she watched them. Serena, knowing exactly how she felt, put an arm around her and squeezed. "It's good to have family isn't it?"

"Yes, it is."

———————— ⌒⌒ ————————

The wedding day started with a low fog covering the grounds of Coeur du Bayou. Serena had slipped quietly out of the cramped daybed she shared with Mason to watch the dawn. Her house and her heart was full. All of the rooms of Coeur du Bayou were occupied except for the yellow room, Anna's room. That room had been designated for the bride and bridesmaids to prepare for the ceremony.

Faith had shown up first, busily finishing up the reception food. Gil had already made several trips, bringing back the food he had kept in his cooler overnight. Claire and the hairdresser had made their way up the stairs to Anna's room. Even Michelle had stuck around to help out. Faith had probably made a dozen trips up and down the stairs already that morning even squeezing in time for her own hair to be done.

Serena stood at the doorway to the event room and smiled at her handy work. Mason, Gabe and Ben had helped set tables and cover chairs. The backdrops had the desired effect and the guests would start arriving any minute.

"Come on. It's time. We need to get dressed." Faith hurried out of the kitchen and headed for the stairs.

"I know. Just checking. One last look." Serena glanced around and was pleased with everything. "We did it, Faith."

"Yes," Faith grinned at her, then snorted. "Well, almost. Come on."

Arm in arm, they made their way up the staircase to Anna's room. Elle and Claire were already dressed and chatting nervously. Michelle handed them their dresses and quickly shooed them behind the screens to change.

Suddenly nervous, Serena slipped the dress on. She had no reason to be. Everything was perfect. The food, the flowers, even the weather seemed to be holding out. As she struggled with the zipper, she heard a knock on the door.

"Hey you guys decent?" Ben called through the closed door.

"Umm. Just a sec." Claire waited for Serena to step from behind the screen. "Yeah, come in."

"Just thought you'd want some pictures in here before we go down. It's almost time." Ben held up his camera.

"Yes, I was waiting to put the veil on her." Michelle smiled at Ben, who immediately blushed.

"Oh, ok." Faith took the veil from Michelle and stood next to Claire in front of the mirror.

"Wait. Serena, you too," Ben instructed. "Claire look into the mirror. Faith on one side. Rena on the other. Elle stand there. If I can get a good angle, this will be sweet."

Ben knelt down turning his camera this way and that while snapping away. Serena caught Claire's eye in the mirror and they laughed. Who would have thought a lost dog in a rain storm would have brought them all together?

"Wow! You guys look great." Ben continued to snap away, giving instructions for their poses.

Holding the camera to his face, he asked casually, "So which one of you is pregnant?"

Shocked, Serena glanced at her friends as Ben clicked the camera rapidly.

"What?" Faith snapped.

"Well, someone in this room is definitely prego." Looking over the camera, Ben watched them thoughtfully. "I've been around Serena and Faith almost every day for the last few weeks. I don't think it's them... Elle?"

"Oh my God, Elleanor!" Wide eyed, Faith turned to her sister. "Is that why you're moving home?"

"No way! It's not me!" Elle glared in Ben's direction shaking her head vigorously.

Finally, everyone turned to Claire who was gazing dreamily in the mirror.

"Oh, hun. Really?" Serena reached out to touch Claire's arm.

"Yes, but don't say anything just yet. I was waiting for the honeymoon to tell Evan." Claire grinned at them, her huge blue eyes dancing.

Amid the squeals and laughter, Serena caught the faint unmistakable scent of gardenias and she knew everything would work out. Evan and Claire would have their promised tomorrow. Jake and Faith's hope for a life together would be fulfilled, while Anna watched on in approval.

Her and Mason... To her, he was her husband already, heart and soul. And even though they didn't need a wedding to prove their love, she knew their wedding would be magic.

THE END

A Word from the Author

Thank you so much for reading Magic: Book Three of the Coeur du Bayou Trilogy.

Wrapping up this series and typing THE END created many strong emotions. I've grown to love these characters and I will miss them. Then I realized it never truly is THE END. The story of the house may have come to a close but these characters continue on.

My next series is about the Del Toro brothers and their ghost hunting team, Spirit Catchers, Inc.

The first book features Elle Bertrand settling into her new job at a local radio station that is rumored to be haunted.

For more information on The Spirit Catchers Series, please follow me on Facebook:

facebook.com/lisacootsauthor

ABOUT THE AUTHOR

Lisa Coots grew up in the tiny Louisiana village of Lacassine, but has always yearned for the challenge of a new adventure. Her youthful dreams ranged from the artistic: as a sketch artist and painter; to the studious: as a writer and librarian.

Lisa's dreams were nudged aside, as dreams often are, by conventional reality. Marriage and motherhood came easily to her and she successfully raised three remarkable children and an amazing husband. When the first pangs of empty nest syndrome came a rapping, she eagerly returned to the artistic passions of her youth; painting, designing, and of course, writing.

Lisa Coots now lives in a slightly larger village in Louisiana with her loving family and lots of furry friends.

LisaCoots.com

www.ingramcontent.com/pod-product-compliance
Lightning Source LLC
Chambersburg PA
CBHW061321200626
46813CB00016B/2558